TO LOVE AND DIE IN ATLANTA

VOL. 2

SA'ID SALAAM

URBAN AESOP PUBLICATIONS

Copyright © 2022 by Sa'id Salaam

All rights reserved.

No part of this book may be reproduced in any form or by any electronic or mechanical means, including information storage and retrieval systems, without written permission from the author, except for the use of brief quotations in a book review.

Email: saidmsalaam@gmail.com

Cover: Adriane Hall

Proofreader: KaiCee White

"I ain't finna go out bad. I wish a bitch would sit here and watch the nigga who kilt my son come and go. All happy 'n-shit!" Marquita growled as she watched Carey junior and his new girlfriend frolic in the driveway. They were supposed to be washing the car but more water was on her shirt than the new car he received for graduation. Carey junior had a shiny new car but all her son got was a shiny new casket.

"You got me all wet!" the pretty girl pouted and poked her thin bottom lip out. Her wet shirt practically dissolved and put her perky, young breast on full display. The pink nipples poked through the fabric.

"I always make the girls wet Becky!" Carey laughed and moved in for a kiss. They made out hot and heavy right there in the driveway as if his parents weren't right inside.

"No! We can't, not here," Becky whined as he rubbed her bare box under the tiny shorts.

"Sure we can! I'm Carey Rollins! I just got away with murder so I can do anything I want!" he declared. He was right too because if a killer gets away with one murder there'll be another one. Which is why he already had two bodies under his belt at eighteen.

"You're right!" she agreed and dropped to her knees right there in the driveway. He was the notorious C-note after all. She pulled his zipper down and came eye to eye with his erection.

"Yes!" Carey declared as his dick disappeared down her throat. It reminded him of feeding time with his boa constrictor. His eyes closed as his head lolled back to enjoy the blow job. It was a pretty good one with her tonsils tickling the head of his dick but the closed eyes prevented him from see the impending danger.

"Wish I could get some head," Carey senior sighed as he watched from the window. His son had a different chick over the house every day but he was stuck with a frigid wife. Sinclair was sucking plenty dick, just not his. His head shook at what had to be done so he reached for his own throbbing erection.

Carey glanced across the street to see if Marquita happened to be outside and saw she just so happened to be crossing the street. He began to smile but the object in her hand wouldn't allow it. He registered the gun just as she looked up and locked eyes with him.

They were her eyes but looked empty inside. Like not connected to her soul. Marquita broke off the eye contact when she reached her victim. There was time for Carey to call out but he didn't. Just watched as the neighbor raised the gun to his son's forehead.

'Psss', Marquita whispered and tapped Carey's head with the barrel of the gun. His eyes opened and went wide with shock. A smile spread on her face just as she tugged the trigger. The car wash was wasted when his brains splattered all over the new car.

The girl spat the dead dick from her mouth and began to scream. She screamed and screamed until she snatched Marquita from her sleep.

"Shit!" Marquita pouted when she realized it was just another dream. She may have awakened from the dream but was still living the nightmare. She looked at her clock and sighed. In a few hours she had to bury her son.

CHAPTER ONE

"Why don't you just go back over there?" Sinclair asked as she startled her husband in the window.

'I should', Carey said in his mind. There, or anywhere besides here with them. He abandoned his post so it was Sinclair who saw Marquita when she emerged from her house.

"Hmp! Looks like she's going to the club!" she huffed at the form fitting black dress.

"Except, she's going to bury her child!" Carey snapped in his friend's defense. "As a matter of fact..."

"What are you doing?" she demanded when he walked into the 'his' of the his and her walk-in closets. He didn't answer since she would figure it out when he emerged with one of his black suits and shoes. "You are not going to that funeral! I forbid it!"

"Forbid?" Carey asked and strained his face as if he didn't understand the word. Only because he did and forbidding is for people in authority. He couldn't pinpoint when he relinquished his authority but knew at that moment he was taking it back. "You don't forbid me to do anything! I forbid and allow around here! I forbid you to forbid anything!"

"Ok," she relented sheepishly. Sometimes a lion has to roar to remind muhfuckas that he's a lion. "You don't have to yell."

"Yes, I do. Because if I don't you don't listen. Now, I'm going to pay my respects to the woman who lost her child because…" he said and stopped short of saying the truth. The truth was they had a killer in their house.

Carey junior hadn't emerged from his room since coming home from the jail. He was spared the worst of it since the county jail here in West view wasn't filled with hardened criminals. Mainly people driving too fast through their jurisdiction with drugs or warrants. He would have been eaten alive had he been put in one of the city jails.

Sinclair was slightly aroused by his assertive outburst but her own ego wouldn't let it last. She watched scornfully as he dressed in a tailored black suit. He looked as good in clothes as he did without him. It took a minute to recall the last time they had sex. It never dawned on her that she was depriving herself in rationing the sex.

"Got a few minutes to spare…" Sinclair purred and crossed her legs seductively.

"Now? Really?" he dared and twisted his lips at the timing. It was transparent though since she just wanted to prevent him from attending the funeral. His head was still shaking as he left the room.

Carey was relieved to see his son's bedroom door was still closed when he came out. He wasn't necessarily afraid of the teen but just didn't want to be around him. He wasn't necessarily not afraid of him either since seeing the smile on his face after the murder. The scene played over and over in his head like a hit song on the radio.

Sinclair already harbored scorn for her husband but turning her down for sex only turned it up a notch. She watched as he stepped out of the house and looked across the street. Marquita's car was still there but he got into his own and pulled away.

"Guess she's on CPT to her own son's funeral!" she huffed and dialed the newest number in her phone.

"Sinclair?" Duane McCoy asked even though the name was on the screen. This was his private line so he mentally abandoned his plans.

"Yes. My husband insisted on going to the funeral for that boy!" she snitched. "Something about paying his respects!"

"What! I told you guys you're the victims! No apologies! No paying respects!" he fussed. For his plan to work Marquis had to be the villain to Carey junior's victim.

"And still he's gone," she replied and paused to see if she really wanted to go there. She did, so she did. "We have a few hours..."

"We're going to need them!" he declared eagerly. "Meet me at the Marriott downtown!"

"MAN..." Marquita moaned when the clock just kept on moving. She needed more time before putting her only child in the ground. Only, there just isn't enough time for that ever so she sighed and stood.

She ignored the buzz of her phone as she stuck it into her

purse. The glass and blood had been cleaned from the driveway but the stain remained in her brain. Even the new car suddenly seemed old when she got into it. Was this what she traded her son for? They were just fine in the hood but she wanted to get out. Just had to get out to the suburbs. Now she couldn't remember if it was for his sake or her own. She was the only one who won. With a new house and new car while Marquis lay in a new casket.

Marquita was on full autopilot mode as she followed the turn by turn directions of the GPS. She was ok with him being buried in the same cemetery as her mama but it was filled to the rim. If nothing was done about the violence in the hood they would fill up another one.

"There she is!" someone announced as she entered the fancy church.

"Right this way..." an usher said in a hush and ushered her up to the front pew. The preacher gave a nod and began the overdue spiel about the teen he never met.

"Hey niece," Marquita's uncle Carlos greeted and gave her a hug.

"Hey," she said and winced at the strong weed scent emanating from him. She had to look down at his hands to see if he was holding a smoldering blunt at the moment. As inappropriate as that would be, she still wouldn't mind a toke or two.

They sat and listened to the white man give the eulogy for the black kid. He proved that love transcends race and brought the mourners to fresh tears. Marquita glanced around the packed pews and realized her son was loved. It was more than just basketball too, he made a lasting impression on everyone he met. Kelondra sobbed on her mother's shoulder while she cried him a river. Mrs Worthington mourned her own son as well as this one. Also dead was her daughter's innocence. The girl could never go back to where she was after what she's been through.

Carey's head was down when Marquita's reached him. He must have felt her gaze and lifted his head to make eye contact. The sorrow in his eyes was genuine since he lost his only son as well. Except he lost him a few years ago. Now he lived with a stranger he didn't know or like.

"Quita?" uncle Carlos asked when he saw her and the man still looking at each other. Both tried to listen to the comforting words but found themselves looking at each other once again. Loneliness will do that to people.

"Huh?" she asked, sounding slightly perturbed at being interrupted until she realized the preacher was finished preaching. Now, the mourners lined up to pay their last respects and say final words. Classmates old and new as well as coaches and players going back to peewee league were in that line. Once they said what they needed to say to the corpse they filed by to give condolences.

"I..." was as far as Kelondra could get before bursting into tears once again. Her mother worried she must be dehydrated from all the tears she shed. Not just today but for the last few months.

"I know baby," Marquita sighed and held her as her mother looked on.

"Come on baby," Mrs Worthington urged and tried to peel her daughter off the woman.

"It's fine. I got her," Marquita said and held on to the girl. Meanwhile Carlos looked down at the teen's ass and legs.

Then checked the mother out for a moment. He preferred the teen so his eyes went back over to Kelondra.

Kelondra rode in the limo with Marquita and Carlos over to the cemetery. It would drop them back at the church once the burial was complete. The women were still huddled up while the man scanned Kelondra from head to toe. He would squeeze one but it wouldn't be appropriate at a time like this.

Marquita was here and elsewhere at the same time. She looked straight ahead during the burial since who wants to see their people get put in the dirt. She passed on tossing a handful of dirt or laying flowers on the casket. Her mind was too busy trying to figure out how to keep on living. Even if it was just long enough to do what she needed to do. Her job would be done and people could throw dirt on her own casket.

"Hey," Carey repeated when the first one didn't get a response.

"Oh hey," Marquita finally replied when finally registering his presence. Meanwhile Carlos looked on protectively from the side.

"You good niece?" he asked since he could sense the awkwardness exuding from them both.

"Yeah, this my neighbor," she told him, then to Carey, "This is my uncle."

"Not the one who..." Carey began to ask but caught himself. Dude had a weird vibe like the kind of man who would peep out the window and masturbate to teens jumping rope.

"Huh? Oh yeah!" she asked and answered. They both shared a laugh that caused a few frowns. She cleared her throat and went back into mourning. "Thank you for coming."

"It's the um, least I can do," he sighed and walked off crestfallen.

"Who is that?" Carlos asked since it was obvious he was somebody.

"My neighbor," she repeated, since anything more would have been too much. Plus, it was just all so confusing. Carey Rollins senior was a nice man. She genuinely liked him but still had every intention on killing his son.

"I'm so sorry," Coach Callahan offered, pulling Marquita back to the present before she slipped into another murderous day dream.

"Thank you," she said to her and everyone else who came to give condolences instead of congratulations. Because there would be no congrats for graduation, college, NCAA bids or first round selections to the NBA.

Marquita wasn't even sure why she was thanking the people for their condolences. Perhaps it was polite but why should she have to be polite when her only child was lying in the box.

The box was lowered into the ground and the mourners went back to their lives. Kelondra rode back with her mother leaving Carlos and Marquita alone in the limo.

"You brang that?" she asked and broke the silence.

"Chill," he replied and nodded up towards the driver. The man would be able to hear any conversation since the car was silent. The radio would be so inappropriate at a time like this. Especially since every other song on the radio is about how some niggas would kill another nigga. Or violate the honor of the women they were supposed to take care of.

No sense banning guns when every song and movie is about killing people.

"Oh, ok," she sighed and understood. Even though she wasn't worried about witnesses since she didn't care about getting caught or getting away. Carlos on the other hand would be just as guilty for providing the future murder weapon.

"Sorry for your loss," the driver offered as he held the door open when they arrived back at the church.

"Me too," Marquita sighed and twisted her lips. Her uncle got out behind her and walked her over to her car.

"Here you go niece," Carlos said in a hush as he produced a pistol from his pants. He glanced in each and every direction as he passed it off.

"You had this on you the whole time!" she shrieked and hurried to conceal it in her purse.

"I stay strapped no matter what, no matter where!" he answered.

"Oh yeah! I 'member when granny got on 'yo head for toting a gun to church!" Marquita laughed. The hearty laugh didn't detract from the weight of the weapon in her bag. Nor the weight of what it meant.

"You know I'll do this for you. Ion care nothing about no chain gang," Carlos confided. He had been in and out of prison so many times the lines had blurred between the two. Freedom and incarceration alternated just like the day and the night.

"I know but, I gotta," she insisted and reflected on the reasons just to make sure she did indeed have to. Carey would be just as dead if her uncle did the deed. The way Sinclair Rollins turned her nose up at her sealed the deal though. She didn't care anything about prison either. At least he would be dead.

"A'ight niece," Carlos shrugged, sighed and hugged her neck. He turned to leave, then turned back for one final question. "Sup with that gal that rode in the limo?"

"Bye uncle Carlos!" Marquita laughed and shook her head before getting back into her car and going home.

CHAPTER TWO

"That Carey is one lucky man!" Duane repeated as he and Sinclair dressed. He was stupid enough to believe that good sex made a good woman. It doesn't, not even close. No more than good dick equals a good provider. There are plenty certified dick slingers who can't or won't take care of their families. Likewise, Sinclair had that wet-wet, monkey grip vagina and still wasn't shit.

"He's lucky to have me!" she seconded as if her lying, cheating ass was some sort of catch to hold on to. She was really for the streets and the sooner he sent her back, the better.

"Well, I'm happy he shared!" the lawyer laughed.

"I'm not his to share!" she huffed with an air of indignation that didn't fit the time or circumstances. Not after being smashed every way but loose over the last few hours.

This was meant to be revenge for her husband's attending the funeral but ole esquire was quite the dick slinger. He was bigger and better than her husband in the sack. Especially since he didn't care about her and fucked her silly like a one night stand.

"On another note..." he was saying but paused to watch her shimmy back into her panties. They came off a lot easier than they came off.

"Another round?" she wondered since she was sexually starved.

"Another time," he decided after a glance at his watch. He actually had an appointment with a jeweler. It was time to pop the question to his long time girlfriend, even if he knew he wouldn't be faithful. He was a lawyer after all and dishonesty ran through his veins. Lawyers are some of the most corrupt and fucked up people on God's green earth. "I had a few incidentals pop up. I'm going to need twelve thousand dollars more."

"Luckily I pulled extra cash! My so-called husband would let our son go to prison!" she huffed and fished the cash from her purse.

McCoy shook his head and cursed himself inwardly when he saw how much more cash she had. He should have asked for more. His shoulders shrugged since he was going to fuck the rest of it out of her too. At least he had secured enough to the engagement ring today.

"FUCK!" Carey senior cursed when he reached the house he paid off with over time and pure grind.

The large house was once something to be proud of. It represented manhood since it was the roof over his family's head. He loved coming home to see his name sake son. Little

Carey junior would drop his toys and rush to hug his dad like he had been gone for months, not hours. Now he sat in the driveway stalling since he dreaded going inside.

"I paid for this damn house!" he shouted and got out. Carey stormed into the house and right into a smoke screen. "The fuck!"

"Chill pops, it's just weed," Carey junior laughed and blew a plume of smoke towards the ceiling. "It's legal in ten states."

"Georgia isn't one of them! And, you're on bond. With special conditions!" he reminded and began recalling them verbatim since his house was used to secure that bond. "Ankle monitor, unannounced check ins, no alcohol, no drugs..."

"No nuts! That's your problem dad, no nuts!" the teen laughed and continued. "If you had a set you would have been smashed that fat ass across the street!"

"You must have forgotten I'm married to your mother!" he shot back in his own defense.

"Who don't give you none!" Carey junior reminded. Even he couldn't remember the last time he heard their bed squeaking down the hall. His father blushed even though he had too much melanin for it to show.

"Never mind our love life. You concern yourself with the conditions of your bond! Or I can just have it revoked!" Carey senior snapped and stormed off just as his sweaty wife returned.

"What was that about?" she asked since she caught the tail end of the outburst.

"Father wants to have my bail revoked! Why does he

hate me so much?" Young Carey pouted and pleaded helplessly.

"Because he is just jealous of you!" she said and rushed across the smoke filled room without saying anything about the smoke that filled the room. She pulled the killer into her bosom and rocked him like a baby. "He knows you'll be twice the man he will ever be!"

"I know mother," the brat agreed and rocked in his mother's embrace. Even monsters love a mother's embrace.

"HMP!" Marquita huffed as she headed down a familiar road. It had been a few months since she made this journey to the central Georgia prison where her baby daddy was housed for the last seventeen years. The trips grew less frequently over the years since they no longer planned to be together once he got out. As of late she only made the trip so Marquis could see his daddy.

"Fuck!" she groaned since this week's mission was to inform him that he no longer had a son. The prison chaplain already delivered the grim news but she needed to speak to him about it face to face. Face time didn't count when it came to matters like this.

"Giiiiirl!" she laughed at the fond memory a nearby gas station brought back to mind. It was the last stop before the prison so she would pull in to use their bathroom. She would stuff her vagina full of balloons filled with various drugs stuffed inside a condom.

Big Marquis would swallow those balloons while bouncing his son on his lap. He made enough money to support his family from behind the wall. Because men are the protectors and maintainers of women, no matter what. Men make ways, not excuses.

At least she didn't have to worry about being searched this time when she joined the long line of loved ones going to see the ones they loved. See recognized some of the same faces she had been seeing over the years. They made innocuous small talk while waiting to get inside. A small commotion in the back made the wait a little more interesting.

"All these Roller hoes stank! That's why all these flies out here!" a young girl proclaimed loudly. The gang usually wore green but the prison had prohibited all gang colors even for visitors.

"Naw, your pussy stank!" the Rider girl shot back. Their boyfriends and baby daddies were at war so they fought every weekend to show their support.

They nearly came to blows until officers intervened. At least they provided some entertainment during the wait to get inside.

"Hey," Marquita greeted and placed her drivers license on the counter. The officer knew her and who she was coming to see so she entered the information without even looking.

"Have a nice visit," she offered and passed her along to the metal detectors.

"Thanks," she said and breezed through the machine. It didn't beep so she was ushered into the multipurpose area of the prison. The large room was host to classes, church and visitation on the weekend.

Marquita thought about everything other than the

conversation ahead as she drove down. The moment of truth came rushing at her when saw Big Marquis. He was just Marquis now that there was no more little Marquis.

'Damn!' Marquita grimaced and bit her lip in her own mind when she saw her first love. He looked more like a twenty five year old athlete than a prisoner in his late thirties. His smooth, dark skin was healthy and glowing. Not having any bad habits were perfectly preserving him. She didn't get to admire it today though because the deep pain etched into it like a sculpture.

"I'm sorry Marquis! I tried to protect him!" she blurted and broke down into heavy sobs. Marquis caught her before she fell and held her. The guard watched carefully to make sure no exchange of contraband happened during the hug. Not that he would stop it, he just wanted in.

"You good?" he finally asked in between sobs and heaves.

"Naw, but I'm gonna be," she decided. The question seemed dry so she pulled away. Both took their plastic seats opposite the plastic table.

"Chaplain had to call me out and tell me my son was dead," Marquis stated but it was a question. He had a cell phone and she had the number. So he needed an explanation.

"Cuz I was too busy tryna wash his blood off my hands. 'Scuse me if I was busy!" she snapped loud enough to get the guard's attention.

"It's not yo fault," he sighed. It hurt so much he needed someone to blame but she lost as much as he did.

"No, it's that weird lil boy's fault!" she snarled. Marquita had kept watch out the window but couldn't catch a glimpse of her target. She looked like the iconic Malcolm X picture, peeking out the blinds with a gun in hand.

"Oh, we waiting on him. Wherever he touch in the system he finna get touched!" he assured. Marquis was loved in the hood so his killer would be killed as soon as he hit the prison system. Not even protective custody would be able to protect him.

"He's not coming. They rich folk. Rich folk don't come to jail," she said as her head shook. The man across the table from her didn't get a bond. No one she knew in the hood got one but the boy who killed her son was home in a few days.

"Shoot me the address then," he whispered across the table. He didn't need to explain the rest because she already knew.

"Check," she acknowledged the unsaid threat that a smirk lifted the corner of her mouth. It dissolved with his next words.

"Whole family finna feel it," he snarled.

"Naw, cuz the whole family ain't did nothing!" she shot back. "The mama ain't shit but the daddy, he a'ight."

"Check," he nodded at the twinkle in her eye when she mentioned the daddy. He knew her since they were eight years old. He was the first one who put a twinkle in her eye. Which reminded him, "Fucked up what happened to Leon."

"That wasn't you was it?" she had to wonder. If anyone knew how long his arms were it was her. Long enough to reach out and touch anything or anyone even from jail.

"Hell naw. Me and Leon was cool. We talked 'fo you gave him some of my pussy," he laughed.

"This ain't been your pussy in a long time!" she huffed

and rolled her eyes. A sly smile still peeked out for a second at the thought.

"Yeah, ole boy fucked up them folks money. He was asking to get whacked," Marquis shrugged. Prison couldn't keep his ear from the street so he knew more about what was happening out there than she did. Her lips twisted at the memory of that night. He did have a pocket full of money for the first time she could recall. "You ain't bring no balloons?"

"Hell naw!" she fussed and rolled her eyes. It had been years since he stopped asking the mother of his child to risk her freedom and their child by sneaking contraband in her box.

"I'm just kidding. Just miss that good gravy on them when I swallow them," he laughed.

"You so nasty!" she giggled and blushed. The rest of the visit was light hearted and upbeat despite them both separately plotting to kill the kid who killed their kid. They separated with a sibling-like hug but he did watch her fat ass until she left the room.

CHAPTER THREE

"How was jail bro?" Bart asked in wide eyed awe. The nerdy black kid had always wanted to hang out with C-note but Keto was his right hand man. He was dead now though and Carey couldn't leave the house so he was up.

"It was..." Carey junior was saying but stopped short of saying scary. They had both seen Sixty Days In set in the notorious Fulton county jail. The West view jail was more like the one in Mayberry but even that would have been too much for the wannabe thug. "Crazy man! I had to put my smack down! A few times!"

"Whoa!" the nerd cheered and pushed his glasses up the bridge of his nose so he could hear better.

"Hell yeah! Jail was crazy bruh!" he continued and laid down another layer of bullshit. The truth was he played up the possibility of a concussion and stayed in the medical unit until his lawyer secured a bail. "I need a favor..."

"From me?" Bart asked incredibly.

"Hell yeah! You're my boy ain't you?" he dared.

"Uh, yeah! Hell yeah!" he agreed eagerly. Good thing Carey wasn't gay because Bart was ready to fulfill whatever he requested.

"I need weed. But no one will bring any to the house," Carey admitted. He was a pariah after shooting the school's superstar athlete. Even the ones who took his side didn't want to go to his house at the moment.

"Weed? Where can I get weed?" he wondered and looked around the room. His glasses slid down his nose again but he quickly pushed them back up.

"Chad has some but won't come over. I need you to go to him," he explained.

"Ok!" he said and got all goofy at the chance to do something nefarious. He accepted the cash and headed out to make his first drug deal. Carey now had a pair of boots on the ground to handle the things he couldn't do due to the bulky monitor on his ankle. "But, I can't ride my bike that far?"

"Use my car," Carey sighed and tossed him the keys. He had gotten Chad to sell him some but had to meet him across town.

"Really!" the nerd gushed and swooned. His parents drove nice cars but he was regulated to his ten speed. Plus, they worked too hard to come up just to give their money away to anyone, including their son.

"Yeah," he reluctantly agreed. He really didn't want anyone driving his car but didn't want to stay sober either. His head shook when Bart bobbled the key toss and scrambled to pick them up.

"My bad!" he gushed and dropped them again. He repeated the instructions once again and a few more times on his way out to the car.

'Do it!' the devil shouted in Marquita's soul and psyche when she spotted her victim coming out of the house. She had made it her new mission to stalk Carey junior from Marquis's old bedroom window. It wasn't his anymore since he was laying in a windowless box six feet under the earth.

Marquita cocked the weapon and rushed around to the side door. She didn't want to alert him by coming out of the front door. It had taken a few days to get this shot and she planned to take it. Carey senior just so happened to look out his own window when he heard his front door open. He needed to make sure his spoiled son didn't blow the conditions of his bond by leaving the house his wife used to secure it. He wouldn't mind the monster going back to jail, but he didn't want to lose his house.

'Do it!' the devil whispered louder and louder until it thundered in her head. Carey recognized her instantly but his eyes were drawn to her hand. Even in the darkness of night the black gun glistened. He was supposed to say something, anything to save his son but didn't.

"Hey..." Marquita called when she eased up on Bart trying to open the car. She wanted to make sure he saw her before sending him off to the afterlife.

"Huh?" Bart asked and spun just before she lifted the gun to his face. It was only then that she realized this wasn't her intended victim.

Even though it was too late since her brain had already sent the command to her finger to squeeze the trigger. Luckily for Bart, his parents, and Marquita the safety was still on the gun. It took a full few seconds before the nerd registered the danger. His eyes went wide as his mouth began to open for a scream.

"Hey guys!" Carey senior called as he came rushing from the front door. Marquita spun and headed across the street in a rush.

"That l,l,l,ady al, al, almost shot me!" the kid stuttered.

"Who? Oh no, that's just, the lady from the home owners association," he quickly came up with. "Gotta change the garbage cans to the new ones. Yeah."

"Wow! They don't play!" Bart gushed and got into the car. He would tell Carey all about it when he returned but Carey didn't pay much attention to his ramblings. Good thing Bart didn't see her return to the home across the street so he couldn't report that part.

Carey senior did though and now wasn't sure what to do about it.

"I'M HEADING OUT!" Sinclair announced as she emerged from the closet. The clothes she wore pretty much said the same thing. Her head lifted in a dare since she was obviously dressed to impress a man.

"Ok," Carey replied, since he didn't care. The short dress and high heels barely registered as she traipsed out of the room. He watched from the window until she pulled away, then looked across the street. He could tell Marquita's car hadn't moved in the days since she nearly murdered the neighbor. They needed to have that conversation but he had no idea how to broach that subject.

"Hey neighbor. Is there any way I can get you to trim your hedges a little, oh and not kill my kid?" he asked his reflection. The ludicrous look on his face made his head shake it off. He couldn't bring himself to go across the street but he couldn't sit in the house with his disrespectful son either.

"Fucking brat..." Carey grumbled as he stepped from his room and had his senses assaulted. The sounds of some good, skin slapping sex wafted on the dense cloud of weed smoke filling the hall.

'Yes! No! Mmhm!' the girl sang along with the rhythm of the headboard hitting the wall. Carey junior was digging her out real good as he headed out of the house. His head lifted like his wife's had done on her way to get laid as he crossed the street.

"Huh?" Marquita wondered when her door bell began to chime. No one came over so it was a rare sound. Marquis used to ring it simply because they never had a doorbell before. It chimed again as she thought about the first one . "Who!"

"It's uh, me. Carey..." Carey was saying as the door pulled open. Carey reeled when a strange woman appeared at the door. He blinked until Marquita came into focus.

"I know I'm looking crazy..." she said and rubbed her head full of hair. She invited him in by turning and walking back into the living room. Carey didn't want to look at her ass but her ass pulled his eyes down anyway. It looked smaller than before but so did she.

"Are you eating?" he had to wonder when he looked into her gaunt face. Her sunken eyes had bags under them since she slept as little as she had been eating.

"Who?" she asked, which meant no.

"I'm going to order some food!" he insisted and pulled out

his phone. He used the S&S Chicken and Waffles app and ordered his favorite combination times two.

"Thanks cuz I ain't..." she was saying until she drifted back inside of her head. Where she had lived in the weeks since losing her only son. Carey just watched from the side, stealing glances at her legs. Time traveled at the speed of life and soon the doorbell rang again. Marquita gave Carey a confused look.

"The food," he said and stood. He fished a few bills from his pocket on the way to the door to tip the driver.

"Thanks!" the young driver cheered since he had been tipped via the app and again in person. Carey grunted and turned back inside of the house. The coffee table in front of the sofa was cluttered so he took the food to the rarely used dining room table.

"Soups on!" he called but Marquita didn't budge. He went to collect her before repeating himself. "Soups on."

"You bought soup?" she wondered since she wasn't familiar with the term. She always learned a lot from their conversations. She picked up age old adages that were new to her along with euphemisms, analogies and double entendres. Likewise she taught him the slang that gave him insight on what his son was saying about him.

"Better than soup!" he cheered as he helped her up from the sofa. He grimaced when he caught a whiff of the funk from her underarms.

"I know I stank!" she fussed playfully and sniffed her underarms. "I cain't seem to get off the couch."

"Well, you have help now. I'll help you," he vowed. He realized she was his only real friend and now she realized the same about him. He did help too by laying out the food in front of her. Even pouring the right amount of syrup on the waffles.

The well needed food seemed to boost Marquita's spirit as she ate. Good food and company will do that. Which is why it's always good to keep good company even if that means being by yourself. It's better to be alone than keep bad company.

"Thank you," Marquita said with a sincerity in her eyes that he didn't get at home. On the rare occasions when his wife or son offered thanks it wasn't very sincere. They were selfish and privileged brats who thought he owed them.

"You're welcome," he said and took up the empty plates. The garbage was full so he pushed it down as much as he could and vowed to take it out when he left. Marquita stood and wobbled slightly since she hadn't done much standing. Carey was a whole man, and men are the protectors and maintainers of women so he sprang into action. "Whoa! I got you."

"Thank you," she smiled securely under his arm. She pointed the way to her cluttered bedroom and into the ensuite. "Scuse my room. I..."

"Been through a lot," he finished for her and reached into the shower to turn on the water. She silently slipped out of the tank top and shorts while he adjusted the temperature. "Here you...."

Marquita got a giggle and blush out of his reaction when he saw her naked. She had lost a few pounds from the grief inspired starvation but it only burned off the extra grits and cornbread. It left the luscious lady curves that took his breath away.

"I'm sorry," he offered, staring but didn't turn away. He

couldn't turn away if he wanted to but didn't want to.

"Don't be," she shrugged and stepped under the steaming water. Carey watched as she lathered a loofa and got to business. She paused to glance at the lump in his Kakis and smiled. "Go 'head..."

Carey locked eyes with her as he retrieved his rock hard erection. He grabbed a bottle of fruity lotion from the counter and squeezed some into his palm. He won the staring contest when her eyes dropped to watch him stroke his dick. It turned her on so much she reached between her legs and cupped her lonely, throbbing vagina.

A finger wiggled at the same rhythmic cadence as he pulled his pecker. She stole glances at him while his eyes roamed up and down her body. Carey couldn't decide where to park his eyes since everything looked good. The plump, heavy breast, hard stomach, round ass and firm thighs. Finally he settled on the pretty face framed by her wet hair.

"Oooh, I'm finna cum!" she warned and frowned. She kept her word too and bust a shivering nut right in her own hand.

"Fuck!" he grunted and sent an arch of semen in the air. It hit her thigh but was quickly washed down the drain by the flow of water.

"That's it. Get it out," she cooed and encouraged as he milked himself dry in front of her.

"I um, I'm sorry, I um..." Carey stammered. It's amazing how common sense returns literally the second a man bust a nut. He scrambled to put his dick away as he rushed from the room. They still needed to have the conversation about the other night but this wasn't the time. He did remember the full garbage can on his way out and took it with him.

CHAPTER FOUR

Carey junior was going for round five when Carey senior returned from across the street. The house was filled with even more weed smoke but he was too relaxed from busting that good nut he just had busted. His knees were still wobbly even if he felt a little guilty.

"Tuh!" Carey huffed in his own defense since he was pretty sure his wife was having an affair. Just as sure as he was that something happened between her and Duane. He knew his old friend was quite a womanizer in college and didn't expect that would change once he became wealthy. Plus he was rumored to be well endowed which was a hit with the ladies.

Still, his values were his values and he felt bad about the encounter. Even if the memory of Marquita's body rushed back to mind and stiffened his dick in an instant. He sighed, shrugged and pulled the lube from his nightstand to beat his meat back into submission. It's easier to fall asleep on an empty stomach than with a hard dick. The moans wafting down the hall helped a porno play in his mind as he tugged and twisted his erection. His legs shifted underneath him as feeling intensified. This was going to be a good one, until it wasn't.

"Don't mind me..." Sinclair laughed as she stumbled into the room. Carey had been so caught up he didn't hear her come in over the music and sex down the hall.

"It's not what it looks like!" he declared and let loose his dick. Except it was rock hard and shiny from the lube so what else could it be.

"Really!" she quipped and lolled her head in laughter. A dry, stinging laugh that deflated his dick along with his ego. The uproarious laughter tipped her over on the bed.

"Are you drunk?" he asked somewhat rhetorically since she was obviously inebriated.

"Drunk and sore thanks to your big dicked friend!" she giggled then turned serious. "Can I say big dicked, or just big dick?"

"So you are sleeping with Duane?" Carey asked professionally.

"Oh, wasn't any sleeping involved. We fucked! Sucked, fucked, then fucked again!" she said in his face. "And, I'll fuck the whole world to save my son!"

Carey wasn't shocked but he was a wimp. He was mad but didn't yell and wouldn't break anything. His wife tilted her head, waiting for a response but he had none. Instead he rolled from the bed and headed for the door.

"You forgot this!" she called after him and threw the tube of lube. It hit him on his back as he retreated downstairs to the den.

❄

"HUH?" Carey asked when laughter pulled him from a pleasant dream. He and Marquita were walking hand in hand on a beach when he was snatched into the present. His eyes opened to see his son and yet another pretty little white girl huddled up on the leather loveseat. He spent the night in the den but his son didn't respect him enough to let him have the room.

Carey junior was always a hit with the girls but the notoriety of the murder case only added to his bad boy persona. The brush with jail had straightened him up for a while but C-note was now back full-time. As a result a dense fog of weed smoke hovered in the room.

"Do you mind Carey!" his father fussed.

"As a matter of fact, I do. I have company and you're kinda in the way!" he snapped.

"In the way? This is my house!" he snapped back.

"See, that whole my house narrative is getting old," Carey challenged. His father's eyes went wide with shock so he continued. "Other people live here, you know? Mom, me. This is our house!"

"Should be!" the bubbly white girl bubbled beside him. One of her nipples fell out the side of the wife beater she wore until she tucked it back.

"You know what..." he relented and stood. He wanted to get out of there before the young girl made his dick hard again. It was still early since they had been up all night using methamphetamines and smoking weed. He still got ready for work so he could get away from these people.

Sinclair was slobbing on the pillow from her long night out. She wasn't exaggerating about not getting any sleep. Duane drug her around the hotel room all night and sent her home to his old friend, sweaty and sore. Carey defiantly made noise as he got ready for work to wake her up. She cursed and grumbled as he left the room and house.

"Hey there!" Marquita called from across the street when Carey emerged for work. She had bounced back from her funk just in time to return to work herself. Deloris had told her to take a few weeks off after the murder of her child. Like a few weeks should cure the grief. It didn't but she needed to be busy again. Needed to see what her new life was going to be head on.

"Hey yourself!" he smiled and crossed the street. Half the smile came from not having to hide speaking to her. Duane told the Rollins family to stay away so made it a point not to. "You look..."

"Better!" she finished for him. She felt better after the good meal, good nut and good bath. It was followed by a good night's sleep that made her wake up refreshed. "You ok?"

"Me?" he had to wonder since she was the one who lost a child. She smiled and nodded as an answer so he answered her question. "Actually, yes. I do have a request?"

"You're my friend Carey. Just ask and I got you! Whatever it is!" she assured him and closed the gap between him. Ninety nine percent of it was genuine while the rest was being catty in hopes his wife looked out and saw her standing close enough to kiss the man.

"Um..." he said, getting stuck on the 'whatever' in her answer. He wanted to take her inside and put her in a sixty nine position for the rest of the day. She smiled at the faraway look in his eyes as he thought about twirling his tongue in her pussy with her lips wrapped tightly around his dick. He had to shake his head tersely to dislodge the thought and get back to his point. "Oh yeah, could you not kill my son. He probably deserves it but you don't."

Marquita just blinked and watched as he walked back across the street and got into his car. She was still standing there a few minutes after he pulled away. Her head turned when movement across the street stole her from her thoughts. The gun was still inside and she braced herself to come face to face with her son's killer without it.

"Must be trash day? I see trash on the curb..." Sinclair laughed out loud but hopped in her car before she got her butt whipped again.

"It is trash day," Marquita laughed since she was the trash who ran her own husband away. It was just a matter of time until she ran him straight into her bed. The thought made Marquita laugh even harder as she got into her car to go to work. "Put some of this hood pussy on ole boy and issa wrap!"

That gave her a good giggle all the way out of the subdivision. The rest of the ride was consumed with her and her married neighbor. They went too far last night but could reel it in and be friends. This she was sure of even if she was sure she wanted more. Her mother wasn't in her life long before the hood claimed her when Marquita was twelve. The woman gave her random rules that made no sense back then but one of them was to never fuck a married man.

'God will get you 'fo that!' the woman used to say. She had committed enough trespasses in life to at least warn her only child on what not to do. The hood hadn't equipped her with enough of what to do but knowing what not to do was still a win.

"I'm ain't mama," she vowed to her mother's memory and

sighed. She blasted the radio for the rest of the way. The mindless music kept her from thinking about anything and that was the point. The same music had most of society not thinking about anything either and that's just fucked up. People are going to need to think in life.

"Oh!" the receptionist reeled as if she was shocked to see Marquita when she walked in.

"Um, good morning to you too Alison," Marquita replied and tilted her head to walk with dignity to her desk. The stunned receptionist made a quick call once she passed.

"Let's get this money!" Marquita encouraged herself as she took her seat. She smiled at Marquis's picture on her desk but refused to be sad. Instead she chose to use it for motivation and make him proud. He played basketball to get her out the hood so she would work just as hard. Except her login wasn't working.

"The fuck?" she asked the keyboard but the keyboard couldn't tell her. She gathered herself and spelled the password out as she typed. "A,T,L,S,H,A,W,T,Y..."

"Um, can I have a word with you? In my office?" Deloris asked as she appeared just as the login failed again.

"Sure, cuz something is wrong with my computer..." she said as she got up and followed behind. She amused herself by looking at the woman's empty dress where a backside should be.

"Have a seat..." Deloris said as she went around the desk to her own seat.

"What's up? I have some catching up to do since I've been off..." she said, hoping to rush this along. All she had left was her work and the new found love of numbers.

"Well, we um. Sorry for your loss again. We just knew

we would make state finals with Marquis," she offered. "But, we assumed you would be, going back now that, you know."

"I know what?" she asked, trying to follow along.

"I mean, you were given the job and car because your son played ball. But now that's he's, well. We figured you would go back to where you came from?" she fumbled along to her point.

It was so plain Marquita caught her point but was still frozen in place. Unmitigated gall has that effect on people. Never in a million years would she think these people would take back everything they gave her after her son was murdered. Only because she was new to this world. This world was as cut throat and backstabbing as any hood or prison.

People used each other as human rungs to climb the ladder. Both men and women married spouses they literally despised if it would help their position in life. After a respectful period they could divorce but used drugs and affairs in the meanwhile to cope.

"I um, ok. Wow," Marquita finally spoke. It dawned on her that not only was she about to lose everything she had, but didn't even have a place to go. "Just, wow!"

"We have put together a gift. A check, to help with the transition," Deloris said and pushed a ten thousand dollar check across the desk. The memo said bereavement since it couldn't say the truth that they were some bullshit.

Marquita looked at the numbers and dipped inside of her head. Deloris wondered if she would have to call security to have her removed from the office. Meanwhile Marquita was trying to figure out her next move. Not long ago ten thousand dollars was a lot of money. Now it was a pittance compared to her account portfolio.

"Ok," she relented and stood. She had recently buried her teenage son so anything less than that was nothing. She collected the check and marched out with her head high. A tear managed to get loose but she knocked it away before it could reach her cheek. Not before it was seen though.

"Marquita? Are you ok?" Harold wanted to know. The older, white man had made her his business when he heard the women cackling about her on her first day. He came from nothing himself and was now the highest earner in the company. With his help she was doing better numbers than those same chickens who were clucking about her.

"Yes!" she tried to say but couldn't. She wasn't ok so she broke down in sobs and told him what just happened. She barely finished her story before Harold yanked her along by her arm. He drug her down the hall and into the boss's office.

"What the fuck is going on around here Deloris!" he demanded as he stormed in without knocking.

"What? I, what did she tell you?" Deloris pleaded. She obviously didn't want smoke with him so she quickly tried to avert the attention to Marquita.

"Told him y'all let me go," she said while Harold titled his head for explanation.

"Well, you were hired as a courtesy because, well..." she stammered but realized how it sounded. She did have a leg to stand on so she shifted her weight to that side. "Georgia is an 'at will' state. Employers do not need cause to dismiss an employee."

"You're absolutely correct. Come on Marquita. Let's head over to Sachs and offer them a package deal for the both of us!" he said and turned for the door. His foot didn't even land on his first step before Deloris literally came over the desk to block the door.

"Wait! Harold, can we talk alone?" she pleaded.

"Nothing to talk about. If she goes, I go," he stated and crossed his arms like, 'how you like me now'. Her face nearly cracked in half so he rubbed it in even further. "Oh, I'm taking my clients with me."

"No! That won't be necessary. We've been a little hasty!" she said steering them back into the office. "Marquita, dear. We would love for you to stay!"

"Me too," she admitted and handed the check back.

"What's this?" Harold wanted to know and plucked it from her hand before Deloris could get it.

"Just a severance package," Deloris explained.

"No, this says bereavement! Very nice of you," he said and gave it back to Marquita. She looked at Deloris who gave a nod.

"Thanks, and I'ma need my login back working again," she said before spinning and marching back through the office.

CHAPTER FIVE

"I have no idea why you're going to this!" Sinclair fussed as Carey dressed. "You know we're sleeping together and I have no intention of stopping!"

"Because Duane invited me and several other friends," he explained since he was the one who ngot the invitation from the lawyer. It was she who wanted to go alone so she could get laid afterwards. But Carey had insight on the reason for the dinner and wouldn't miss it for the world. The actual invitation was for him, she was the plus one.

"Tuh!" she huffed and refused to give him props on how he looked in his new suit. She was underdressed in the tiny dress that made her battle to keep both breasts in at the same time.

"You look..." he began and the sucker for compliments perked up and paid attention. Carey didn't finish though and walked away. His name sake son was dressed for a night out as well. Which begged the question, "Where are you going?"

"Out!" C-note shot back. He sounded tough to his dad but folded slightly when his mother came out of the bedroom. "I'm going fucking crazy in this house! I need to get out!"

"I know, baby. Maybe you can get out for a few hours," Sinclair cooed and relented.

"We can lose the house if something happens!" Carey reminded but neither of them were swayed. They never contributed a dime towards the house and weren't moved.

They haggled over how far he could go and how long he could be gone while he took action. He marched down to the kitchen and selected one of the expensive knives his wife had purchased. A large butcher's knife got the call and he stepped out to the driveway. He politely slashed all four of his tires and went back inside.

"Are you coming with me or not?" Carey demanded to his wife but didn't wait for an answer.

"I haven't come with you in twenty years of marriage," she mumbled loud enough to hear as she followed him out to his car. She noticed the tires and immediately knew who did it. "That woman slashed Carey's tires!"

"No she didn't. I did," he corrected and got inside the car. Sinclair paused like she was unsure what to do until he started the car. When he shifted it into reverse she hopped in the passenger seat.

"Just childish!" she fussed and crossed her arms over her chest. She refused to buckle her seat belt as an act of defiance to him. Meanwhile he fantasized about running into walls and embankments the whole way over to the bar. She berated and verbally abused Carey the whole ride to the restaurant but he was unfazed. Instead a smirk lifted a corner of his mouth at what he knew was coming. "Just because I rode here with you doesn't mean I'm riding back with you."

"Yeah," Carey agreed and pulled up to the valet. His head shook at the fact that his money was paying for this lavish dinner. He was greeted by other friends from school that he hadn't seen since school.

"Hey Carey Rollins!" they cheered and he would call their names back. They would hug and slap backs and exchange business cards even if no one planned to stay in contact anymore than they had been.

"See, this is class!" Sinclair said snidely as they stepped into the piano bar and restaurant Duane McCoy rented for the event. "As much money as you make and we don't do things like this! What do you do with all of our money!"

'Paid off a half million dollar house. Paid cash for cars, shopping, saved for retirement...' he thought but didn't say.

"Yes dear," he sighed and took their seats. Dinner was served while Sinclair searched the room for her lover. She had several drinks before, during and after the main course.

"Ladies and gentlemen, welcome your host to the stage..." an announcer announced as Duane came out.

"Thanks for coming out!" he greeted and launched into his virgin standup comedy routine. He made enough money in his professional profession that he could pursue his passion on the side.

'Stick to your day job', Carey thought inwardly while clapping and laughing graciously at the corny jokes. Sinclair whooped, hollered and cheered loudly to the dry jokes and bad timing. She was drunk though so some of it was funny to her.

"Hey thanks guys! I really appreciate you all for coming out! This is a really big night for me, but it's not just about me," he sighed and switched gears. "Hailey, can you please come up?"

"Me?" the busty, bubbly white woman gushed as she rushed the stage. She was as bad an actor as he was a comedian and it seems staged. As staged as the exaggerated haste that made her breast bounce as she took his side.

"What's going on?" Sinclair asked and squinted as Duane descended to one knee.

"Looks like he's about to pop the question?" Carey chuckled as he produced a ring. His wife let out a gasp as Duane did just that.

"Yes! Yes! Of course I'll marry you!" Hailey cheered, cheesed and bounced her big breast some more. Duane beamed brightly as he stood and claimed his prize. He had finally made it and a big titty, white wife to prove it.

"Guess he's gonna cut his mustache off next..." Carey snickered as he waited in the line of friends to congratulate the lawyer. Sinclair stayed back tossing back more drinks.

"Hey there buddy! Thanks for coming," Duane greeted and hugged Carey like he hadn't been fucking his wife. It was free pussy since Sinclair threw herself at him. He was done with her now that he had his white, trophy wife.

"Wouldn't have missed it for the world!" he laughed and looked Hailey up and down as they embraced.

"And don't worry about Carey junior. I spoke with the district attorney..." he said and concluded the sentence with a wink. The law had very little to do amongst the rich and powerful. Which is why OJ was able to kill two people and get away with it while Sa'id Salaam got convicted of something he didn't do.

"Oh, ok," Carey nodded. The sooner this was over the

better but his heart went out to Marquita. She would be deprived of the justice she deserved for her son. His head hung as he headed over to collect the wife he was beginning to hate. "You ready?"

"Yes, as a matter of fact I am!" she slurred, stood and wobbled slightly from all the alcohol she consumed. She ignored the hand he extended to help her and swaggered over to some man at the bar. Carey just blinked as they walked out of the bar together.

"WHAT NOW?" Carey said when he saw police cars as soon as he entered the subdivision. He was actually happy Sinclair left with a stranger so he could go spend time with Marquita. Even if they didn't do what they did last time he still enjoyed her company.

The thought crossed his mind that he might be rolling up to yet another murder scene. Marquita could have killed his son and he honestly wasn't sure how he felt about it. Whatever it was had something to do with his son. That much he was sure of and was confirmed when he saw the flashing lights in his driveway. His head turned and saw Marquita standing on her porch watching. He wanted to go to her but Carey was calling his name.

"Dad! There's my dad! Dad!" Carey junior called and pointed at his father before he could get away.

"Oh damn!" he sighed and pulled up. "What's going on here?"

"We got a call from the monitoring company," reported a breach.

"I just went to the store you moron!" the brat snapped at the cop.

"The GPS said you went to Atlanta," the other cop corrected.

"How?" Carey wondered and looked over at his son's car. It still had the four flat tires he gave it before they left. That's when he noticed his wife's car had been moved. "Oh."

"Mom said I could go!" Carey shouted at his father. That's when he noticed she wasn't by his side. "Where's mom?"

"Um..." Carey senior paused. He was pretty sure what she was doing, just not where she was doing it. Actually Sinclair was folded in half in a motel twin bed with a stranger digging her out. He was fucking her fast and furiously since he had to get home to his own wife.

"We picked up the GPS when he got back to West View but he refused to pull over," the first cop whined. He then held up a bag of fluffy green buds. "Then found marijuana in the car."

"So, I guess you have to take him in?" Carey shrugged since he was cool with it. He looked back across the street at Marquita looking back.

"Well Mr Rollins..." the senior cop sighed and looked around. "We'll write it up as a glitch. It just can't happen again. You understand, young man!"

"Yes sir," Carey junior said, proving he could be contrite when he needed to be. His father just shook his head as his son got yet another slap on the wrist. It was the free passes, looks the other way and wrist slaps that turned the kid into a killer.

"Let's ride," the older cop told the younger. They both turned to get back in their cars to leave.

"You dropped something," the younger one said and dropped the bag of weed in the driveway.

"Un-fucking believable!" Carey exclaimed as his son collected his marijuana and went inside. He looked back over at Marquita just before she too went inside and closed the door. He let out a sigh and retreated to his bedroom and went to bed.

"YES!" Carey demanded when he took Sinclair's call late the next morning. He was enjoying the peace of not waking up next to her until she rang his line.

"I need you to come get me!" she demanded as if she had a right to demand anything. He was here dealing with the crisis while she was getting her back blown out.

"From where?" he blurted before the better question came to mind. "Why?"

"Why? Because you drove me last night! Which means my car is at home! Why, is because I'm your damn wife!" she barked.

"My wife who left in the arms of some strange man last night," he reminded. Not that he really minded since he didn't want her. He just didn't know how to get out of this financially intact. Divorcing wealthy men was the suburban equivalent to playing the numbers in the hood.

"Um, he's not strange to me! Robert, no Wilbert, and I are friends!" she shot back.

"Then why doesn't your friend bring you home?" he

asked. He should have been asking if she and Carey junior could go live with whoever this Robert or Wilbert whose name was actually William.

"Because, he had an emergency!" she shot back in his defense. Even though he had actually crept out after dicking her down real good. His own wife didn't play that, spending a night out so he washed his dick in the sink and rushed home.

"Sure," Carey sighed and caved in. Only because he was a wimp who let his family walk over him. He may have been a shark in the boardroom but he was a hoe at home. Which is still better than those men who get treated like bitches in the street yet roar like a lion in front of their family.

His head shook as he dressed to retrieve his wife from a drunken orgy. Then shook again when he ran into a haze of weed smoke in his house. Once more when he came face to face with a topless white girl. His eyes locked onto her bouncing breast until his son spoke up.

"She'll let you hit dude," Carey junior offered. He and the girl cracked up when he blushed and rushed out of the house. His head shook once again at being run out of his own house. "Come back and get some head!"

"You ok?" Marquita called from across the street. The distress on his face was visible that far away.

"Huh? Yeah, I'm..." he replied as he went over. He took notice of the sundress she wore instead of her infamous tiny shorts. "Um, fine."

"You sure?" she asked because his face said anything but fine.

"No," he said and lifted his chin. He wasn't fine and wasn't going to pretend anymore. Instead he confided in his friend the events that got him here. There was no mention of Carey junior and his escapades but Marquita surmised it for herself last night.

"Wow! So, she got her face cracked by the lawyer, then went home with some nigga from the club?" she recapped.

"And now needs a ride since he left her," he added.

"And you finna get her?" she reeled with a hand on her hip. Carey just blinked because of how crazy it sounded out loud. "Why don't you just leave her?"

"God knows I want to. Want to leave them both," he admitted. It felt like a ton of bricks lifted off of his soul just saying it out loud. His lips twisted as the rest of it came to mind. "I just don't want to leave everything I've worked so hard for."

"You mean stuff? You finna be miserable over some stuff? Life ain't but this short..." she said, holding her index finger and thumb together. "And you finna waste yours over some stuff!"

"That simple huh?" he asked as he turned to leave. He hated to admit it but it really was that simple. You're gonna leave all that stuff behind when you die so why die over that same stuff.

CHAPTER SIX

"Shit," Carey senior cursed when he saw four new tires on his son's car. He knew he paid for it since his family were deadbeat freeloaders. Sinclair still had access to the household account containing thousands of dollars. It was now short a thousand dollars courtesy of those four new tires.

Carey junior was pushing the limits of his ankle monitor further and further. Just proof you can't let people get away with shit or they'll do some more shit. His father felt the hood of the car on his way in to see if it had been used. It was still warm since he just pulled in from swapping one girl for the next.

"Of course!" he fussed when he walked into the smoke-filled house. Voices and laughter wafted from the den from his company. His son couldn't go party so he brought the party to him.

"Don't bother them!" Sinclair warned when she saw her husband's face.

"Bother them? I live here!" he reminded. "And, no one is

going to live here if Carey keeps violating the conditions of bond. The ankle monitor is so he doesn't leave the house!"

"He's eighteen! He needs to get some air," she protested. Carey just tilted his head and wonder if she was just crazy or just plain old stupid. She had to be one or the other so now he just wondered how he missed it.

"We'll have plenty of air when we're sleeping under a bridge!" he sighed and headed up to the room. By the time he finished in the shower she was gone on her date. Not that he minded since it gave him the chance to head across the street.

"Come in!" Marquita called out in reply to the doorbell. Carey came in wearing a smile since she was wearing a nice dress and heels. "Oh, hey Carey."

"Oh? Expecting someone else?" Carey asked through the same smile. It was meant as a joke but she didn't laugh.

"Um, actually, I um, kinda have a date," she admitted sheepishly. They hadn't repeated or even talked about their mutual masturbation but the date came as a surprise.

"Oh, um, ok. Yeah, ok," he stammered. He tried to be cool but the pain was etched on his face. "A date, that's um, yeah, great?"

"I'm sorry. I can cancel if..." she was saying but Carey was used to disappointment.

"No, go. Have fun!" he insisted. He cracked a smile but it didn't match the look in his eyes. It was as incongruent as new shoes and old clothes. The doorbell rang interrupting the debate.

"Come in!" she called back over towards the door. Carey turned and watched as Harold entered the house. He wasn't sure if he should be worried or relieved to see the older white gentleman.

"Hey there Marquita! Are you ready?" Harold greeted warmly as he entered.

"I sure am," she beamed and made the introduction. "Harold, this is my neighbor, Carey Rollins. Carey, Harold."

"Nice to meet you!" Carey offered full of enthusiasm. He heard about what he did to save her job and liked him already.

"Likewise!" Harold said and gripped his hand. "Will you be joining us? This one claims she's never been bowling!"

"Um," Carey hummed while Marquita looked to him for his answer. Bowling would be fun but he was relieved to see her date was an old white guy. His mind then went to the house full of teens across the street and decided to babysit. "No, I'd better stay home."

"See you later?" she asked and waited for an answer

"Sure. Sure you will," he smiled. Harold smiled too since he had a genuine interest in seeing her happy. Some people just like seeing everyone happy. Harold was some people.

"Where are you going?" Carey demanded when he came home just as Carey and his friends were leaving. He blocked the door to the house he stood to lose if his son violated the conditions of bail.

"Out!" he snapped and tried to go around his father.

"You're not going anywhere!" he insisted and put his foot down. Not far enough since his son shoved him aside and went out with his friends.

※

"GET UP!" Sinclair demanded and shook her husband's shoulder when she came in from her date the next morning.

"Huh? What!" he asked then reeled when he smelled stale alcohol and dick on her breath since she was breathing down his face.

"Your son was arrested last night! We have to go get him!" she fussed on her way into the closet to change.

"Why?" he replied to the first sentence but it applied to the second as well. Carey was relieved his murderous son was out of the house. Not to mention him being in custody saves the house his wife put up for bond. He looked over as Sinclair pulled her dress off and saw she wasn't wearing the panties she left with.

"Why? Because he's your son! You know what..." she fussed and moved even faster. He did know what but didn't know what she would do without him being there so he rolled out of bed and scrambled to get dressed.

A few minutes later they both emerged from the house. Carey senior twisted his lips at the empty space where Carey Junior's car would have been if his wife hadn't bought four new tires. She even sprang for new rims for the inconvenience. Why not since she was spending her husband's money. The purse she carried was loaded with the extra cash she pulled out for the incidentals.

Both Mr and Mrs Rollins looked across the street and saw Marquita's car was still parked out front. He had fallen asleep before she and Harold returned from their night out. He didn't expect his car to still be there and it wasn't. Sinclair pulled her phone, then changed her mind.

"You need to call your friend!" she demanded once they were seated in his car.

"I do?" he asked and cast another glance at Marquita's house.

"Not that friend you idiot! Your lawyer friend! The one with the new fiance," she said and rolled her eyes.

"Oh, ok," Carey replied and smiled inwardly at her distress. Carey junior had used his one phone call to call his mother. Luckily she was riding the man she went home with and saw her phone ringing on his night stand.

"Put him on speaker. I don't trust you," Sinclair insisted. Carey nearly bit on it but didn't. Instead he compiled and ran the call through the vehicle's speaker phone system.

"Carey?" Duane asked when he took the call. He almost asked what was wrong until he remembered that spoiled ass son of his. "Let me guess, Carey junior violated his bond conditions."

"Again," he sighed and filled him in on the first time.

"Sheesh. This is going to cost," the lawyer sighed and doubled down. "This won't be cheap!"

"She already put my house up against the five hundred thousand dollar bail!" Carey moaned.

"No, that will remain the same if I can get the judge to reinstate the bond," he corrected then clarified. "My fee. This is going to cost!"

"I don't have, I can't get, have access..." Carey pleaded. His wife had already dipped a heavy hand into their retirement accounts.

"I have twenty thousand on me!" Sinclair leaned in and announced.

"That will get me started. You can owe me the other half," McCoy said and began to get dressed himself. Life is good when it takes twenty racks to get you to put your shoes on. He liked Carey even if he was slightly jealous of him in college.

People just liked Carey because he was genuine. By anyone's account he was a nice person. Which is why his wife ran all over him. Once Duane saw that he decided to take advantage of him and run the check on him as well. He fucked his wife and charged him double to do it. He even billed him for the first visit when Sinclair gave him a blow job in the living room.

Sinclair handed the lawyer the money in the courthouse parking lot. Duane used his connections to get before a judge before Carey junior was taken to the county jail. He whispered in the prosecutor's ear that made his head nod. Whatever he said cost him five of the twenty thousand dollars and the state put up no objections to having the bond reinstated.

"Young man this is your absolute last chance! If you violate your bond again you will sit in the county jail until the resolution of your case," the judge boomed down from his perch. "Now stay out of trouble!"

"Yes your honor," Carey junior said contritely. Carey actually could stay out of trouble but C-note couldn't. In fact a whole heap of trouble was heading his way.

"HOW'S MY FAVORITE CSI TECH!" Johnson asked as he entered the Atlanta police lab. He had a fling with her once upon a time which worked for or against him, depending on her mood.

"Which one?" another lady tech asked as she came out of

an office. He had a thing with her too since he liked to spread it around.

"Both! Together, separately, either way I can get it," he laughed. They didn't though.

"Won't get this again!" the black one huffed and twisted her neck like only black girls can.

"Barely got this!" the Asian one laughed. The two techs cackled and high fived at his expense. Not that he really cared since he had conquered them both and that's what mattered most to men like him. Each woman was like a mini Mount Everest to him. He just wanted to mount them all and plant his flag.

"Ha, ha. Glad you ladies are having a good time but, anything back on that MLK boulevard shooting?" he asked. A white tourist had been murdered in the hood so this had priority.

"Yup! Same gun was used in another couple of robberies," the Asian of the two said.

"Kids I bet," the black lady guessed since the victims were all shot in the leg. The robber was no killer since he was shooting his victims in their legs. Including this white one who just happened to bleed out. He was a killer now.

"They'll be old men by the time they come up for parole!" Johnson bet. That was only if they got life with parole. His lips twisted at the revelation that this shooting was part of a larger crime scene.

"Oh! I got a hit on your ghost gun too!" the black of the two remembered. "The gun used in the prep boy shooting out in West View was used in the murder of Manuel Cole."

"Aka, Man-man..." Johnson added and nodded since he was familiar with the name. It was just one of many unsolved murders in the dangerous city of Atlanta. "See you guys later..."

"Not if we see you first!" the Asian laughed and initiated another high five.

"Sup?" Latisha asked when her partner came back looking perplexed. "Burning when you pee again?"

"Everyone has jokes today," he sighed. "That Cole gun was used in another shooting."

"So what else is new?" she asked and twisted her lips. It wasn't uncommon for one gun to be linked to several crimes across the city and surrounding counties. Used guns used in crimes were passed around the hood like STDs.

"Worth checking out," he said and got an eye roll from his partner. "Or, I can."

"You should. I'll check out the surveillance footage in the tourist case," Latisha replied.

Johnson would much rather trace a gun through the city than hours of boring security footage. He pulled up the interdepartmental database to review the murder of Marquis Williams. Even he would have bit on the self defense angle they were pushing. Carey Rollins was a good kid from a good family.

"And yo mama is fine!" he laughed when he pulled up pictures of the Rollins family. Mrs Worthington wouldn't return his calls but he loved the clean suburban wives who did dirty things in bed. "At least worth a trip..."

CHAPTER SEVEN

"Sure you don't want me to come with?" Latisha asked as her partner grabbed his files to head out to the suburbs.

"Nah, follow up on the MLK case," he declined. Johnson assumed this was a wild goose chase but had to turn over all leaves and rocks to clear the cold case. From what he read the Rollins kid was a wannabe drug dealer. His guess was Carey probably bought the hot gun from the hood after his friend got killed.

He didn't expect much but needed to go alone so he could stalk Mrs Worthington while he was out there. It was creepy but she had some really, really good coochie so he didn't mind. The drive out of the hood was introspective. He could have lived out here in the suburbs. His salary could stand it, but he had an entirely different retirement plan in mind. He had bought a small villa in the Dominican Republic with it's booming sex trafficking. There he could live out the rest of his days in bliss and licentiousness.

"Nice," Johnson admitted when he entered the subdivision where the Rollins family lived. His eyes shifted left and right and took in the symmetry. All the lawns were manicured and clean. Even the trash can were perfectly aligned as if there were some sort of contest.

A stark contrast to the haphazard hood. His block was lined with splotchy lawns with bare spots and broken down cars. Packs of wild dogs roamed and ravaged trash cans on the street. Occasionally a stray hooker might ramble by and save him gas from going to pick one up. He would get serviced in his car port and never invite them inside.

"Shit..." he said when he realized he passed the house. Several blinds had cracks in them to watch the unknown vehicle back up. The neighborhood didn't have a neighborhood watch but the neighborhood still watched.

Johnson pulled behind Mrs Rollins' car in the driveway and got out. His detective skills went to work and he peeped in both cars as he headed up to the front door. His face scrunched at the smell of weed seeping through the closed door. It was so incongruent to the neighborhood that he smelled his own shirt to make sure it wasn't him.

"Carey! Are you expecting company?" Mrs Rollins called up to her son when the doorbell began its song. He actually did hear her over the thump of his music since he only cranked it when his father was home. He was just fucked up like that and got a kick out ignoring his parents. She let out a sigh and went to answer it herself. "Can I help you?"

"Perhaps. I'm detective Johnson from the Atlanta homicide division," he began and paused to show his badge. "I'm hoping Carey can help me with a case I'm working?"

"He will definitely cooperate!" she immediately replied

and called him again. He ignored her again so she went to collect him. "Please have a seat. I'll get him."

"Thank you," he said and headed for the sofa. His shin hit the coffee table from his watching Sinclair's ass as she rushed away. He was a detective so he jotted his observation in his pad. "Mrs Rollins got a fat ass!"

"Whaaaat!" Carey fussed when his mother barged into his smoke filled room. "Don't you knock!"

"A detective is downstairs! He needs your help and you're going to help him!" she demanded. She would have put him in a headlock and drug him down if need be. "Helping him will help your case!"

"Ok," he relented since this latest brush with jail hadn't worn off yet. He was ready to get these five years on probation his lawyer was negotiating.

McCoy knew the spoiled brat wouldn't be able to fulfill the conditions of probation any better than he was the conditions of his bond. Carey junior would definitely and repeatedly violate probation over those five years. Then he would hit his old friend over and over again to keep his son out of prison. Reinstatements, rehab and diversion centers would net him another hundred grand from the family.

"Detective..." Sinclair was saying as she produced her son. She had already forgotten his name since she had been gone.

"Johnson," he reminded and stood to greet Carey. He decided to treat him like a witness instead of a suspect so he extended his hand. "You must be Carey?"

"Yes. Carey Rollins junior," he said formally and respectfully. He was just C-note a minute ago while listening to the latest drill music. He knew how to turn it on and more importantly off, when necessary.

"Don't worry, you're not in any trouble. I actually worked your friend's case," the cop said and glanced down at the pad. "Kenneth Worthington. We arrested everyone involved."

"Thank goodness! That was just terrible!" Mrs Rollins reeled and swooned. She wanted to sip her vodka but would wait.

"It was. What I'm wondering about, and maybe you can help me?" Johnson said and paused for effect.

"Sure! Anything!" he eagerly agreed.

"The ghost gun. The one your friend had, where'd it come from?" he asked. Carey flinched so imperceptibly even his mama who birthed him missed it. The trained detective did not and leaned in.

"Keto, I mean Kenneth ordered the parts. He had a guy who assembled them," Carey said, saying more than he knew he said.

'Them. He said them?' the detective noticed. He knew to keep quiet and the suspect would keep talking. Carey had just talked himself into being a suspect.

"Yeah, I told him to be careful around Man-man and them guys..." Carey rambled.

'He knew my vic! Oh shit, this kid is my killer!' Johnson screamed in his mind while staying calm and collected on the surface. He cast a slight glance to Mrs Rollins and noticed an even slighter strain on her face. Women know their kids and she knew her kid was lying.

"Ok, I thought maybe you guys bought the guns from Man-man and Scooter ndem," the cop casually offered. The plurality was a test that included the ghost gun he used to murder his neighbor. If there was no break in the chain of custody between the murders than this kid was a murderer.

"No, Kenneth made them. I..." Johnson was saying.

"Maybe we should have his attorney present?" Sinclair interjected when she heard the strain in his voice that came when he was lying. He was telling the truth but the truth hid another truth he wanted to lie about.

"No, that won't be necessary. I have everything I need," he said amicably and stood. Mrs Rollins stood with him.

"I'll walk you out," she offered and ushered her son back up to his room. She waited until they were at his vehicle before speaking again. "My son is a good kid!"

"I don't doubt that. But..." he sighed at the obvious. He left it at that since he didn't want to tip his hand. She may have known her son was being deceptive but had no idea he murdered a drug dealer in the city.

"But what?" she offered along with herself since she stepped forward to erase any respectable distance. "I'm trying to keep my son out of prison. I'll do anything!"

"Anything?" he asked and leaned in so their bodies touched. He didn't give a fuck about Man-man and would gladly trade his murder for some more good, clean suburban pussy.

"Everything!" she assured and gripped his dick through his slacks. Johnson smirked as his Johnson got hard in her hand. He took her number and promised to call her later. Once he pulled away he made a call to his partner.

"Anything?" Latisha asked when she took the call.

"Dead end. I spoke with him and his dad. The kid didn't know shit," he said and traded the cold case for a hot body.

"I'M HEADING OUT," Sinclair announced and lifted her chin defiantly.

"Ok," Carey quickly agreed since he preferred his own company to hers. He preferred Marquita's company over his own and planned to cross the street as soon as she pulled away.

Carey senior had gotten into the new routine of checking the Ring can footage after seeing the murder. Seeing your own son kill someone can have that effect on a person. He had also used it to see what time Marquita had returned from her night out. Even strained his eyes to see if she gave Harold a good night kiss. He played the video in fast motion so he could get across the street that much sooner.

"Oh?" he asked when he saw the car drive by, back up, and pull into his driveway. He listened curiously as the cop introduced himself.

'I'm detective Johnson from the Atlanta homicide division. I'm hoping Carey can help me with a case I'm working?'

"Hmp?" he hummed when the cop entered his house. He waited and watched for the twenty minutes it took before the cop came back out. He watched as his wife practically molested him at his car. When she grabbed his dick it explained why she didn't say anything about the visit.

"Carey?" Carey senior asked as he tapped on his son's bedroom door. He realized he was being a wimp again by knocking so softly and put a little more into the next knock.

"The fuck?" C-note wanted to know when he snatched the door open. "The fuck dad!"

"The cop who came by? Is everything ok?" he asked. He cared more about his home than his son at the moment.

"Yeah, some bullshit about Keto. It's all good," he replied and waited. His father stood there trying to put the pieces together but C-note didn't have time for all that. He closed his door and resumed talking to the next chick into delivering some pussy.

Carey shrugged and headed out of the house. He shot a text over to announce himself and Marquita was pulling the door open when he arrived.

"Hey!" she gushed and beamed as an indication of how happy she was to see him. She even squeezed into a tiny pair of shorts and halter top to show as much skin as possible. She respected his marriage vows but also knew he liked to look at her. He was her only friend so she made sure he had plenty to see.

"Hey yourself," he replied and licked her luscious body with her eyes. His eyes were pulled to the plump mound between her legs. After seeing her naked he knew it was all sauce no floss. She had a fat vagina, ass and breast under her clothing.

"Well come on in!" she said and turned inside. She smiled knowing his eyes were locked onto her jiggling ass as they made their way over to the sofa. "Drink?"

"No thanks," he declined since her company was more than quenching. "How was your date?"

"It was great! Bowling is fun! We gotta go sometime!" she gushed.

"We can," he agreed before nodding his head and agreeing with himself. Why couldn't they go out and have fun. Sinclair had no problem going out every night, why should he. Carey had drifted away but Marquita quickly snatched him back down to earth.

"He ate my pussy when he dropped me off," she admitted, then cracked up at the look on his face. "Just playing."

"Well don't," he said forcefully. A little harder than intended so he explained. "Because I have feelings for you."

"Wow!" she exclaimed. Not because she was surprised, but because no man had ever said those words to her. She felt the same but held back from saying it. Not that she needed to since he already knew.

CHAPTER EIGHT

Meanwhile, Sinclair wasn't holding anything back. She gripped Johnson's large Johnson and gnawed up and down the shaft like it was a corn on the cob. Then took it down her throat before repeating the process. He let her enjoy herself for a few minutes before holding her in place and literally fucking her face. 'Gawks' filled the hotel room each time he touched her tonsils.

"Mm-mm!" she protested and shook her head when she felt his body begin to jerk from the impending orgasm. The denial removed consent so he loosed his grip on her head and she loosed the dick from her mouth.

"Fuck!" he grunted as she finished him off with her hands. She stroked his dick until he exploded on her bare chest. She used both hands and wrung him dry like a beach towel after a swim.

"Hoping you'll return the favor?" she asked as she lay back and spread her legs.

"Don't mind if I do..." he said, marveling at her marvelous vagina. His last conquest had a beat up box that looked more like roast beef than pussy. Roast beef is only good to eat on a roll so he passed and just beat it up.

"Yessss," Sinclair hissed and arched her back off the bed as he twirled his tongue. Now she returned the favor and gripped his head. She wrapped her legs around his neck and rode his face like a bucking bronco.

"Mmhm!" he hummed with a mouthful of muff as she began moaning and writhing. He didn't mind letting women come in his mouth though and held on.

Sinclair was literally off the bed as she rode his face. He had to show off a little so he stood straight up. She braced her hands on the ceiling and nutted in his mouth and goatee. He tossed her on the bed and climbed between her legs. These married women weren't prone to be burning so he slid into her raw.

"Damn volcano!" he fussed and grimaced at how hot her box was. It wasn't a complaint though because no man ever has complained about a vagina being too hot or too tight. Hers was both so he took long, slow strokes to enjoy every inch of it.

"Yes!" she purred and enjoyed every inch of the dick he drug in and out of her. He mixed it up a little and rocked from side to side. Sinclair tried to fight the feeling but that only made her come harder. She would come a few more times until that hot lava finally got the best of him.

He debated back and forth as to whether he should bust in her, on her belly or try to get back into her mouth. Debated until it was too late and he exploded inside of her. He pressed his entire weight on the dick and pushed to the bottom of her box and let go. The night was young so there would be plenty of opportunities to explore those other options. By morning he would have conquered them all.

Sinclair kept her word to do everything to keep her son out of jail. In return he agreed to bury what he uncovered about the ghost gun to keep Carey junior from being charged with another body. Her body for his and a fair exchange is no robbery.

"SO, ANYTHING EVENTFUL HAPPENING? HAPPEN?" Carey asked when he shared space with his wife in the same bed. They kept their distance like male cousins having to crash together, except from laying head to toe.

"Like my period?" she wondered in case he was feeling frisky.

"Oh God no!" he grimaced at the thought. He accepted she was for the streets and planned to move once they moved past this situation with their son. "Carey told me a detective from Atlanta came by?"

"Tuh!" she laughed since Johnson did more than come by. He came in her a couple times during their night together. Not that she minded since her period was now on. He could do it again if it kept her son out of jail.

"The cop?" he repeated since she had drifted into her head.

"It was nothing. I took care of it," she dismissed and walked off. Carey twisted his lips and tried to recall when his sorry wife ever took care of anything, ever. He would twist his lips completely off his face before he could answer that.

"I'll find out for myself," he shrugged and pulled up the video footage again. He assumed he was who his wife was screwing now but it was clear they didn't know each other before that first visit.

A quick search for the detective returned several Atlanta newspaper reports of the murder cases he worked. Pictures confirmed he was the same man who came to his house. He skimmed a few cases until coming across a familiar name. The report showed a picture of Kenneth Worthington in better times, when he was alive.

"So, what would that have to do with Carey?" he wondered. He accepted he wouldn't be able to figure it out on his own so he picked up the phone. The homicide division's number was posted on several of the articles so he dialed.

"Atlanta homicide..." a woman announced, sounding bored.

"Detective Johnson please?" Carey requested in his professional voice. There was a pause while she checked the board to see if he was in the office or available. Those were two different things.

"He's out of the office now. Would you like to speak with his partner detective Adams?" she asked helpfully. There was so much pressure to solve the tourist murder she wanted to make sure nothing got by.

"No, I'll um..." Carey was saying while entering the name. A picture of Johnson and Latisha Adams changed his mind. "Yes, please."

"I'll connect you now," the now unbored woman said and transferred the call.

"Detective Adams," Latisha barked briskly to set the tone.

She had no time to waste but the reward was generating a bunch of calls that only wasted her time.

"Detective my name Carey Rollins. Your partner was recently at my home. He spoke with my son and wife..." Carey was saying, not sure where he was going. Meanwhile the astute detective had already entered the names into her computer.

"Yes! How can I help you?" she asked with renewed enthusiasm. Her partner claimed it was a wild goose chase but perhaps the father had something to add.

"I'm not sure? I'm not exactly sure why he was here?" he asked as his answer. There was a brief silence as they both plotted their course. Carey didn't have much so he offered what he did have. "My son is on bail for a um, a manslaughter charge. Your partner thought he could help him with another case?"

"And, you didn't speak with detective Johnson?" she asked and squinted. She was quite sure her partner mentioned speaking with the dad. Johnson lied a lot but generally about some pussy or to secure some pussy or something to do with some pussy.

"No. I was at work. He spoke with my wife, Sinclair," he replied.

"Is your wife there now?" she asked and twisted her lips. Johnson had mumbled some excuse to get away before he left and this could be why. Latisha twisted her lips dubiously when she pulled up a picture of Mrs Sinclair Rollins. She was pretty and shapely which was just how her partner liked them. He took them ugly and unshapely as well but this piqued her interest.

"No. I..." Carey replied.

"Stay there please. I'm on the way!" she said on her way to the exit. Johnson had lied to her before and it usually had some woman involved. She didn't have a dick to think with or slow her down. This could be nothing or it could be everything. Either way she was going to find out.

CAREY SMIRKED at the smell of weed floating through his house. It generally pissed him off but knowing a detective was on the way to the house made him giddy. The thought of his son getting arrested warmed his heart. It would be one down and one to go as far as he was concerned. His trifling wife was busy swallowing Johnson's johnson while he waited on his partner.

'Wyd' Marquita texted from across the street. Carey went over to the window to peep while he responded.

'Waiting for a detective' he said as she appeared in her window.

'Tuh' she replied and closed the blinds. She didn't blame him for his son's actions but any mention of the case pissed her off.

'I'll stop by when she leaves?' he texted back but got no reply. Marquita preferred a man tell her what he was going to do than to ask. He would have to figure that out on his own.

A car pulled up and into the driveway before he could leave the window. He and Latisha made eye contact through the windshield before she stepped out. She was prettier than he expected and had a nice frame in the slacks and blouse.

'That's a detective' Marquita quickly texted and made him smile.

'I'll stop over when she leaves' he shot back and headed down to answer the chiming doorbell. His son's door opened letting a cloud of weed smoke roll into the hallway.

"If that's Jennifer, send her up," C-note demanded like he ran things around there.

"That must be some really good weed if it's got you high enough to believe I work for you!" he laughed and rushed down to let the cop in. He pulled the door open and stepped aside. "Come in."

"Did you forget I was coming?" Latisha quipped when she walked into the smoked filled house. She really didn't care much about weed but was big on respect. Smoking weed when you know a police officer is on the way is the exact opposite of being respectful.

"No, that's my son. He's a thug," Carey replied and turned towards the steps to call.

"One sec!" she urged, to have him to herself before speaking to Carey junior. Plus she wanted to compare notes with the sparse notes her partner offered on the visit.

According to Johnson he spoke with Mr Rollins and Carey junior. No mention of Mrs was made in his report. He claims Carey claimed to finding the gun the same day of the Williams shooting. No connection to Man-man nor Kenneth Worthington.

"If you have to take him in for the weed I understand. Conditions of bond and all..." Carey offered and got a curious look from the cop. She had run into plenty of parents who were fed up with their fucked up kids but the reports showed the Rollins were spending big to spare their child.

"I work homicide," she corrected and continued. Meaning she didn't care anything about weed. "Do you know where your son got the gun used in the incident here? You obviously keep guns in the house, for protection?"

"Uh, no. And no," he replied even though she was nodding her head in the affirmative as she asked. The tactic worked so well she usually accepted the answer. She accepted this one and moved on to the next.

"Did you know your son sold drugs? Him and Kenneth?" she asked with more nodding. Once again it coaxed the truth out.

"Yes. I had a pretty good idea. Why? That's a mystery. He has everything. I know because I gave it to him," he sighed.

"Where's your wife now?" she asked abruptly since sudden lane changes kept subjects off balance.

"If I had to guess I'd say with your partner. I'm pretty sure they're seeing each other," he admitted. That too nodded her head since it confirmed at least one of her suspicions. It could explain the lie so she was ready to speak with the son.

"Can you call Carey down now?" she asked politely.

"I could but he won't come," he said and stood to get him. Generally she wouldn't want to allow suspects to speak so they couldn't match stories but had a feeling the father and son weren't on the same page. She did make use of the time and started the recording program on her phone. Carey knocked and opened the door to his son's bedroom as he was taking dick pics for one of his girlfriends. "Put that away. There's a police officer here to see you."

Carey huffed and blew his breath at the interruption but

didn't put up a fight. The last thing he wanted was his bond revoked so he dropped C-note and took Carey Rollins junior with him.

'Psshh' his father hissed at the transformation as he passed.

"You must be Carey junior? You look just like your dad!" Latisha gushed and stood. She extended her hand and watched his eye shoot down to her chest for a split second. That was good since it told her which way to go with a suspect. Men who lusted even while in trouble were tricks who could be easily tricked into telling on themselves and or others.

"Yes. So I've been told. You won't hold that against me will you?" Carey replied as he shook her hand. His father twisted his lips at his son turning on the charm. He wanted to be proud that his son had picked something up from him but they were beyond that.

"How could anyone!" she fawned. If she hadn't been doing this job for as long as she had been she wouldn't believe for a moment that this kid killed a fly. No wonder the bad boy versus good boy/self defense theory would work for him. Only thing is she had been doing this for a long time. She's seen husbands kill wives, wives kill children and siblings killing siblings. There really wasn't much she hadn't seen during her time as a detective. The world went crazy and she had a front row seat.

"How can I help you?" he asked as they all sank to the sofa. Latisha watched his eyes follow her legs as she crossed them. The move worked a lot better when she wore skirts but she still had his attention.

"Well, my partner and I investigated the death of your

friend. We're just curious about the ghost guns? Where did you guys get them from?" she asked eagerly.

"Keto, Kenneth ordered them both," he quickly replied since it was the truth.

"Ok cool. One for each," she cheered and nodded. "Did anyone else get one?"

"No ma'am. We were the only ones to have them," he nodded proudly.

"Ever loan yours out?" she asked casually but Carey senior saw through it when she leaned in to listen closely. The way her eyes narrowed told him this question was important. He would have advised him not to answer without a lawyer present but didn't want to help him. He killed a kid for no reason and didn't deserve any help.

"No ma'am," Carey replied like a responsible gun owner. Meanwhile Latisha nearly lost her cool. If there was no change in custody of the weapon then she was looking at a cold blooded killer.

"Ok, thanks. That's all I have for now," she said and stood. She watched his eyes run up and down her body as she did.

"Glad I could help," the teen said and headed for the stairs while his father walked her out.

"Is everything ok?" Carey had to ask because her demeanor changed so suddenly.

"Yes. Mmhm," she agreed and smiled with her lips pressed together. Afraid the truth might slip out if she opened them. Latisha Adams got into her car while Marquita watched from her window. The detective pulled away and made a quick call.

"Tell me you arrested someone in the tourist murder? Anyone!" the district attorney pleaded when he took the call.

"Not yet but I did close a cold case. I'm on the way back to the city," she said as she exited the subdivision. "I need a warrant for Carey Rollins junior, first degree murder!"

CHAPTER NINE

"What's going on? Where we going?" Johnson asked in response the Latisha suiting up to make a bust. He had been missing in action from all the action he was getting lately. His newest conquest was a sex starved suburbanite with a vicelike head game named Sinclair Rollins. "The tourist murder?"

"Actually, no. Made a break on the Cole case," she offered and zoomed in to gauge his response. They may have taken a few dollars here and there but this was going too far. He was ready to let a whole killer skate on a body just because the mother had a nice body.

"Oh? Ok, cool! I'll ride with..." he said and donned his own vest. Latisha watched his face and he was still smug. He assumed they were going to arrest someone else for the homicide. Someone who hadn't done it and he was cool with that.

"Where, where are we going?" he asked as the convoy turned onto the expressway in the direction he had headed every day as of late.

"West View," she said and watched from her peripheral

for a reaction and got one. His head snapped in her direction with so much force he nearly spun it around. He grabbed for his phone but his partner wasn't having it. "Call her and I'll have you arrested for obstruction!"

"Huh? Who? I..." he stammered and looked around like he wanted to get out of the car. Luckily there were no stop lights on the expressway because he would have hopped out.

"Mmhm! I can't believe you!" she fussed at him as he sank into his seat. "Was the cat that good?"

"Huh?" he asked, meaning yes. The cat was that good, possibly the best he ever had and now he was on the verge of losing it. His phone buzzed on his side and he looked at it along with his partner. He hit the screen to take the call while saying, "Ignore."

"Mmhm," she said and shook her head again.

"So, what put you on the Rollins kid?" he asked offhandedly. "You have found something good if we're on the way to arrest Carey Rollins junior right now."

"You did. You lied about talking to the dad. As soon as I saw the wife I figured she was the reason. I still went out to follow-up," she began. Johnson just nodded along so she continued. "Anyway, he swears there was no change in control of the ghost gun. That means he had it before and after Cole was killed. Phone records put him in the damn living room when Man-man got killed..."

"Carey! Carey!" Sinclair shouted as she ran up the stairs and into her son's bedroom.

"What mom!" he groaned and tried to pull the comforter over his head.

"Get up!" she demanded and snatched it away. There

was no time to waste after hearing the detective's conversation in the car. "The police are coming to arrest you!"

"Why mom! Make them stop!" he whined as he got out of bed. Carey scrambled to dress while his mother sawed at the ankle monitor with a knife. "Ouch!"

"Man up!" she shouted and kept going. The plastic band gave away and she tossed it aside. Carey tried to pack but there was no time for that. "No! Go!"

"Ok mom!" he shouted back as she rushed him out of the house.

"Take my car! And give me that! Go to the zoo. Park, get out and walk. Don't stop walking until I pick you up!" she fussed and swapped car keys and snatched his phone. She waited until he pulled off before getting into his car.

Johnson looked straight ahead and pretended not to notice Sinclair's car zip by on the other side of the road as they headed to the Rollins home. Carey's car was pulling out of the subdivision as they entered but all eyes were looking ahead to the target house.

Latisha was sharp enough to spot Carey's car pulling out but didn't stop it. She knew she had the element of surprise since she kept the arrest a secret until the last minute. An empty feeling swept over her when she saw the empty driveway. She almost whipped around to give chase but pressed on to the Rollins house but it appeared to be a woman behind the wheel.

The Atlanta cops piled out of their cars and fanned out around the house. This was a murder suspect so guns were drawn and pointed at the house. This was Latisha's raid so she took the lead and pounded on the door.

"Atlanta police! Warrant!" she shouted and banged on

the door with her flashlight. She repeated the process a few times before giving the nod to another cop. That other cop walked forward with the battering ram and knocked the door off the hinges. He stepped aside so the police could swarm inside.

"Police!" the police screamed as they rushed into the house and spread out. Each took a room and announced 'clear!' when they came up empty.

"Looks like they just left?" a cop suggested when he felt a half full cup of coffee. It was still warm when he felt it. "In a hurry too!"

"Mmhm..." Latisha hummed and twisted her lips at her partner. Johnson just shrugged like he didn't know what was going on.

"The kid is on a monitor isn't he?" one of the cops recalled and got another sigh out of Latisha.

"I didn't notify the locals. These rich folks are a different breed," she said in defense of her own breach of protocol. Rules said to notify the proper department but she decided against it. She didn't like how they allowed Carey junior to literally get away with murder. He had been reinstated twice already.

"Let's get a ping on the monitor before they get too far!" another cop suggested and did just that. The other cops toured the half million dollar home while they waited.

"Un-uh! Don't take anything!" Latisha warned her crew. She knew they liked to help themselves to trinkets and whatever they could find. She also took a little pity on Carey senior who seemed overwhelmed by it all. She dealt with enough victims to know the man of this house was one. A victim of both his son and wife. It's crazy when one's own family can be an enemy.

"Got a ping! I-20, east bound," a cop announced and they fled the house as quickly as they had entered. The convoy followed the leader who had gotten the GPS signal from the company. Now they were able to follow the monitor in real time. The target switched to 75/85 then did something odd. "Pulling off, North avenue. It stopped on Spring street."

"Is that, the Varsity?" Marquita wondered at the familiar location. She wondered why a murder suspect on the lam would stop for burgers.

"Them shits are good!" Johnson nodded. He had done his part and tried to help Sinclair but if Carey was stupid enough to get caught buying food that was on him. He should still be able to fuck.

"Personally I prefer S&S Gourmet Burgers but, whatever," she said as they swooped in and surrounded the suspect car.

"Hands! Driver, step out with your hands high!" the police shouted. They didn't get a reply so they kept shouting commands and inched forward. Closer and closer until close enough to see the car was empty. The GPS signal was maxed out meaning they were right on top of the monitor.

"Shit!" Latisha fussed when they opened the door and saw the cut monitor on the floor. "Spread out!"

"He's gone!" a cop said but looked around anyway.

"Yeah he is..." Johnson laughed as his look around spied a familiar ass rushing up Spring street. He knew Sinclair and Carey had switched cars and led them on a wild goose chase. He would still get caught, just not at the moment.

"WHAT NOW?" Carey groaned when he pulled into the subdivision. He knew the heavy police presence had something to do with his family. The neighbors gawking confirmed it before he reached his house and saw cops everywhere. Including a police helicopter hovering above. Police cars were parked where his wife and son's cars would be.

"Mr Rollins?" detective Graves asked when Carey opened his car door. He made it a question even though he knew exactly who he had been waiting for.

"What happened now?" Carey asked instead of answering.

"Where would they go? Your wife and son?" the cop asked instead of answering his question. Carey was so relieved a smirk crept into the corner of his mouth. The detective furrowed his brow and twisted his lips at the incongruent reaction. This was a serious matter yet he seemed elated.

"I honestly have no idea," Carey replied believably enough for the detective to buy it and move on to the next question.

"How much cash was in the house? Did your wife recently withdraw any funds? Did you?" Graves asked and added a twist to see if the husband was in on it.

"Don't know, not sure and hell no!" Carey replied while pulling out his phone. His eyes lifted to see Marquita was one of the curious neighbors watching the Lifetime movie play out in real time. They dropped back to the screen as his banking app opened up. "Hmp..."

"What?" the cop asked and leaned forward to see. Carey

pulled his phone away so he couldn't see but told him anyway.

"She just cleaned out the household account," he realized. It was the only one she had access to after nearly decimating their retirement accounts and signing the house away for bond.

"How much?" Graves asked since it mattered. The right amount of money can get you lost for good. The wrong amount and that ass is caught.

Except in the case of the hillbilly sheriff deputy in Alabama who sprang her boyfriend. She had a hundred thousand in cash but it didn't do them much good. When there was no video of them catching a flight to a non extradition country it was just a matter of time. The dude was six foot nine inches which makes it difficult to lay low. His dumb ass was spotted at a car wash, washing a stolen truck. It begs the question why an escaped convict needed to wash a stolen truck but he was a dumb ass and dumb asses are going to do some dumb ass stuff. It's just what they do.

"Not much. Around eight thousand dollars," he said since that's what it took to maintain the diva and the brat.

"Eight grand..." the detective repeated and pondered. He knew Sinclair wasn't street savvy but knew enough to leave the phones in the cars when they dumped them in the hood. Both cars were promptly stolen by local thugs. Those thugs got the surprise of their lives when police helicopters assisted in the stops. Two surprises actually since cops left them with the cars after ascertaining they weren't the fugitives they were hunting. Neither car was reported stolen so the cops left them in them.

"So, if they're not here..." Carey asked and glanced across the street. The cop followed his eyes and understood.

"We'll be clear in a few minutes. Just trying to get an idea of where they may have gone," Graves explained. He had barely put the period at the end of his sentence before Carey walked away.

"They ran huh?" Marquita asked when he walked over. She had been at work all day herself but it wasn't hard to tell. She still had the gun and still kept an eye out for his son from time to time. Fate was on his side since she couldn't muster up enough nerve to kill him like when she nearly shot Bart.

"Looks like," he replied and couldn't help but smile. She shook her head but smiled as well. They both knew nothing was separating them from being together no except the foot and a half between them.

CHAPTER TEN

"Hey!" Sinclair called out the window when she spotted her son. He wasn't hard to spot on this side of town. "Driver, stop for my son!"

"Ok," the young white guy responded and pulled over. The college student blew off all of his classes when Sinclair shoved five hundred dollars in his face to drive her around. Especially since his old beater probably wasn't even worth that much.

"Mom!" he cheered just like he used to do when she picked him from daycare. It seemed like only yesterday but today he was a double murderer on the run.

"Are you ok?" she asked as he climbed into the car.

"Couldn't you find a better car than this! What is a, Datsun?" the brat complained and she knew he was ok.

"Hey! You're the one who needs a ride! Not me!" the driver protested in defense of his vintage hooptie.

"Don't mind him. He's just stressed," she purred and patted the driver's leg. He was aiding and abetting a fugitive so it was wise to be nice to him.

"Where are we going mom? Are the cops going to get me? Are..." the scared kid rambled. This was the first time his mother wished he really was C-note so he would shut the fuck up.

"Carey!" she shouted so he would shut the fuck up but it was too late.

"Listen, I don't want anything to do with any cops! I'm a student. I..." the driver protested and looked for a place to pull over.

"My son is..." Sinclair began but stopped short of calling him stupid. Another plan came to mind when she saw a used car lot go by the window. She waited a block before speaking. "Here's another hundred to not have seen us. Just let us out here."

"You got weed?" Carey asked when he spotted a roach in the ashtray.

"Just some personal," the driver admitted and held up a small sack of pretty green buds.

"I'll give you two hundred bucks for it!" Carey shouted and reached.

"Sold!" he shouted back and passed off the sack.

"Pay the man mom," Carey instructed and took the weed.

"Really?" Sinclair sighed and parted with even more money. It was the price she would have to pay to save her only child. There was no price she wouldn't pay to save him.

"Where are we going? I'm tired of walking! I'm hungry! I..."

"I need you to hush! Be quiet! I'm trying to save you and I need you to be quiet!" she finally snapped. If she had done this years ago they wouldn't be in this position. They arrived at the lot a few minutes later and purchased a used car for a few thousand dollars. A few hundred more got a dealer plate and the fugitives headed west. With little money and no plan.

"I CAN'T BELIEVE we're actually doing this!" Marquita reeled and giggled as Carey helped remove her shoes.

"We're doing this," he said looking up into her eyes. They both cracked a smile as he began helping her into her bowling shoes.

They had taken the plunge and went out on an actual date. It may have been just to the bowling alley but it would count as their first date. He proudly drove across the street to pick her up just like a real date since she said she never been on one before.

Big Marquis used to take her for take out but tonight was her first sit down dinner at a real restaurant. It wasn't particularly fancy but didn't have a drive through and that was plenty fancy for her. She enjoyed the low murmur of voices mixed with dings and clinks of silverware and glasses. What she enjoyed most was feeling like she belonged. Her head nodded at the suburban folks and realized she was one of them. Her son had given her a better life even if he didn't live to see it.

"Hey..." she called to make him look up from tying the shoe. She popped a kiss on his lips as soon as he did.

"What was that for?" he asked so he could do it again and get another one.

"For everything. For being a friend when I needed one the most!" she said and fought not to tear up. She lost that battle but didn't mind. It felt wonderful to finally be able to be vulnerable and soft. To be a woman instead of the hybrid 'vagina-men' society created by forcing women to play every role in the household.

"Well, I should thank you too," he said and returned the kiss. They knew right then some good, gushy sex was in their immediate future. "I had no idea how miserable I really was until you came along."

"Yeah, cuz yo wife some bullshit!" she cackled.

"Tell me about it," he agreed and mentally transported back to a time when she was the love of his life. Sinclair was once a down ass chick who held him down in every way. He was the sole recipient of all that good sex she was now passing out like pamphlets. "Stay like this. Don't switch up on me."

"Ion know how to be nothing but me," Marquita shrugged. The woman had a lot of attractive features but her personality was the best of them. That's saying a lot too because that ass was fat and perfectly round. Just as round as the softball sized breast, hard stomach and calves. The long, natural hair, slightly slanted eyes, smooth skin and white smile were nice but being genuine trumped all that.

"That's what I love about you," Carey admitted. It may not have been cool for men to reveal emotions but he wasn't concerned much about cool. Marquita squinted at what he was saying. It was as close as she ever came to a man telling her he loved her. Not far-fetched since this was her first real date.

"I love stuff about you too," she said, tilting her head like it was a dare. It was now out in the air so they moved on to their alley and bowled the night away. The touches, hugs and pecks they stole along the way was a prelude of the sex to come.

A SMILE SPREAD on Carey's face when he saw his empty driveway. He picked Marquita up from her house but pulled into his driveway when they returned. Marquita enjoyed having doors opened for her but was in a hurry to get inside of his house to get him inside of her. That would have to wait since they stepped out to find someone waiting.

"Detective Adams?" Carey asked although he was sure of the name. Why she appeared out of nowhere was the real question. He looked around and still didn't see her car parked up the street. Which was exactly as she planned.

"Miss Williams?" Latisha asked but it wasn't much of a question either. More like an acknowledgment of the obvious when she saw the twinkle in Marquita's eyes.

"Yeah we..." Marquita began to explain but it wasn't why the cop was here so she didn't wait.

"Do you have any idea where they might have gone?" Latisha asked even though she knew the answer to that question too.

"No. Could literally be anywhere. She wiped out the checking account after she left," Carey shrugged. He had secured the rest of the accounts but left Sinclair access to the household account. "Just under nine thousand dollars."

"Hmp?" the detective huffed at how nonchalant he seemed about the whole thing. In truth he was relieved to be rid of the both of them. He would have gladly paid the nine grand for them to leave. Little did he know it would cost him a lot more than that. "Can't run for long on that. Does your wife have family anywhere?"

"Virginia," he quickly responded before the rest of that story twisted his lips.

"What?" the detective asked when she detected more to the story.

"I really doubt they would go there. Sinclair isn't really close with her parents," he explained without explaining how she looked down on the hardworking farmers. She scorned the working class even though it was the sweat of her daddy's brow that sent her to college. Then her husband's hard work that moved them up to the upper middle class.

"Well, if you hear from them," Latisha began but left it there since she knew he wouldn't. Everything she knew about the woman said they wouldn't last a week on the lam. The sentence hung in the air as she cast a glance at Marquita and cracked half a smile to show her approval. She knew her partner was fucking the mans wife so she was glad to see he had moved on. Latisha had walked back to her car as the couple walked inside of the still ransacked house.

"Dang!" Marquita exclaimed at the chaos. She had been in a drug raid or two back in the hood and knew the signs.

"I guess they thought they were hiding under the sofa cushions," he said and took her hand. Carey decided to tackle putting the house back together room by room. He had started with his own room so it was pristine when they walked in.

"Dang!" she repeated at the contrast. Plus he had removed every trace that Sinclair was ever there. Her clothes were bagged in the garage even though he doubted she would return for them. Carey stayed focussed on the matter at hand and began to undress. "Oh yeah!"

He laughed as she scrambled to join him naked. They met in the middle of the bed and began to make out. Both of their hands scrambled to touch, caress and fondle each other's body. She gripped and tugged his rock hard erection while he ran a finger in and out of her slippery box.

"Oh!" Marquita squealed when he flipped her on her back and lifted her legs high. She braced herself for the dick but the tongue came first.

"Mm-mm," Carey hummed when he found the pussy was just as sweet as he suspected it would be. It had been a decade since he had dined below the waist but it's just like riding a bike. Even easier perhaps since a bike doesn't moan and writhe to let you know you're riding it right. Marquita sure did and let him know.

"You eating that pussy boy!" she hissed and pulled her legs even higher. He just added to the things she loved about him when his tongue twirled in her twat like a twister. Then added another when he made her come.

Carey hadn't had any head even longer than he had any sex but could wait for her to return the favor. He scrambled up face to face as she cavernously sucked her own juices from his mouth and tongue. He lined up the dick and plunged inside.

"Shit!" he grunted when he felt the vice-like grip of her hot box around his dick. He searched for a stroke but it was not to be. That good hood pussy snatched him by his ankles, held him upside down and shook all the coins from his pockets. "Shit!"

"Mmhm, I know," Marquita laughed and rubbed his

back. She clamped her walls down and made him squirm. The quick nut didn't bother her since he was kind enough to get her off first. Plus, it would take a while to get accustomed to pussy this good after two decades of frigid Sinclair was and her sophisticated vagina.

The couple ignored the puddle they created and cuddled up. This could be their life and they were here for it. Nothing needed to be said so nothing was said. They held on and drifted off to sleep. A good sleep because they were going to need it.

CHAPTER ELEVEN

"Dang!" Marquita exclaimed and shook after Carey redeemed himself the next morning. He lifted her leg and slid that morning wood in from the side.

Marquita turned her head to kiss him and he dug deep and fucked her real good. The sounds of squishy pussy and skin slapping mixed with the chirping birds outside the window. A squirrel ran up the tree in search of a nut but he wasn't the only one.

"You, finna make, me, cum!" she whined in protest. Not that she didn't want to, she just liked to announce it. Carey took heed and dug down even deeper, harder, deeper. Marquita kept her word and let out a howl as she shivered and shook from the strong orgasm.

He wasn't finished yet so he flipped her on her back and lifted her legs to his shoulders. Marquita knew she was in trouble but it was good trouble so she gripped the sheets and gritted her teeth. Carey plunged back inside of her and bungeed off the bottom of her box.

Marquita just looked up at him while he closed his eyes

and drove it home. She was so turned on by watching his face contort from his pleasure she felt another orgasm creeping up her legs. This one would be mutual as they both exploded as one. Married men don't pull out so he pushed in and let her have it. Carey let her legs drop as they kissed and writhed together in post climatic bliss. No telling how long they would have laid there like that if no one had come along and banged on the door.

"That gotta be the police knocking like that!" Marquita declared. She would know since she had been in spots where the police came knocking and that's how they knocked.

"But why?" he wondered as he rolled off of her and the bed. Marquita smiled as he pulled on his pajama pants and headed out. She claimed the pajama shirt and pulled it over her body.

"Sheriff department!" a sheriff deputy called through the door as he pounded. It was his last time before forcing the door. Luckily for the door Carey got there first.

"Surely you don't think they returned?" Carey fussed indignantly as the officers barged past as soon as he opened the door.

"We have orders!" the main deputy announced as the others spread out to search.

"Got a female!" another shouted when he came across Marquita in the bedroom.

"That's my neighbor!" Carey shouted and tried to go up but was detained.

"I'll check," a female deputy said and rushed up the stairs. Once she checked Marquita against the picture she had she was cleared to leave the room. She gathered her clothes and came down stairs in the pajama shirt.

"What's going on?" she asked as she joined Carey in the living room.

"Not sure?" he replied and posed the same question to the deputy. "What's going on? He's not here. She's not here!"

"We know and that's the problem. Your problem..." he replied and handed him the documents. Carey could read just fine but he still explained. "You used your house to secure bail. Bail has been revoked and your son is a fugitive."

"And you're seizing my house!" he reeled as he read the seizure notice. "I'm calling my lawyer!"

"Good idea. Just do it from the curb. This house is now county property!" the deputy said and escorted them outside.

"BUT, BUT, BUT..." Carey interjected between excuses as he spoke to Duane McCoy. He made some compelling points but none pointed to him getting his house back. He was standing in Marquita's window looking at the boards on his door.

"The house will be sold at auction by the time you prove Sinclair forged your name," he assured. "You acquiesced when you came to court and agreed to have it reinstated."

"So there's nothing I can do?" he asked and lifted his chin with dignity. He had learned by now that life has valleys and peaks, wins and losses. Either way, keep your chin up. You can't control what curves come your way but you can control how you deal with them.

"Turn your son and wife in before the seizure hearing," stated, then offered the alternative. "Other than that I've arranged a time for you to collect your personal property from the house."

"Two days..." Carey sighed and drifted into his head. His prissy wife and punk ass son could be anywhere so he didn't know where to even begin. He realized he was alone on the phone and dropped it from his ear.

"You can live here, with me." Marquita offered proudly and lifted her chin as well. Dignity is contagious like that but so is indignity. That's why you have to be so careful about who you let in your life.

"I could," he nodded in agreement. He had an idea but it was a long shot like a three legged horse in the Preakness. The number was deep in his contacts so he pulled it up and called.

"It's Carey!" a woman's voice announced as the call was accepted. The murmurs were muted by a hand over the receiver for a moment before a male came on the line. "We haven't heard from her."

"Yeah, I didn't think she would come there," Carey said since he knew the disdain Sinclair had for her parents. The small town country bumpkins were an embarrassment in the world she wanted to fit in. The FBI had paid them a visit by then so they knew what was going on.

"Yeah, well..." her father said, alluding to the fact that he was ready to get off the phone.

"Yeah," Carey agreed. He certainly couldn't tell him everything would be ok because he was pretty sure it wouldn't be. If anything he guessed it would get worse before it got better. Both men hung up without a goodbye since nothing was good about it. Carey just twisted his lips before muttering, "Where could they be?"

"WHERE ARE WE?" Carey junior asked when he awoke in the moving car. He had smoked himself into a good night's sleep while his mother drove all night.

"Texas," she declared since it was the last state line she crossed. The border was next if she beat the APBs and BOLOs with their names and faces on them. Luckily for them most fugitives were pretty basic and stayed local. The All point bulletins and be on the lookout for notices circulated around the city they had left long behind.

"I'm hungry," he fussed at the woman who had just thrown her life away to save his. He seemed to notice that when her jaws clenched in reply so he changed his tone. "Let's stop for food and change places. I'll drive while you get some rest."

"Now you're talking!" she said and surveyed the signs they passed. She hadn't had to eat fast food since getting married but quickly accepted it would be her only option at the moment. At that point one spot became no different from the other so she pulled into the next burger spot.

"I hate..." Carey began but caught himself. Her sacrifices were bigger than his burger preference so he switched gears. "Every other burger joint but this one!"

"Hmp!" she huffed. It was too little too late to save their lifestyle but she had to save his life. Even she knew her son was soft and would be eaten alive in prison. Many parents lose a son to the system only to have a daughter come back after getting turned out. Or a drug addict, weirdo or mental patient. Some have to come collect their child's corpse. She would not be one, not if she could help it.

Carey kept his word and took over the driving once they ate their fill of burgers and fries. He waited until his mother leaned back and began to snore before lighting more weed. He exhaled a sigh with the first toke since he had no idea where his next sack was coming from. He knew how to find out but his mother had taken his phone. It had only been a day but the withdrawals are similar to coming off heroin.

"Fuck it," Carey decided and looked over to his mother to make sure she was still asleep. She shifted and stirred as he pulled into a gas station and came to a stop. He only pushed the door up so he wouldn't wake her and went inside. "I need a phone."

"Got prepaid..." the clerk said and pointed to the array of cheap phones. Carey selected one from his old network and paid for it and a phone card. He turned and got the surprise of his life.

"Are you ok?" Sinclair asked in response to the look on her face.

"Huh?" he asked and pulled the phone behind his back. Luckily his mother had a pressing agenda of her own and didn't catch it. "Fine."

"Great!" she said and turned to the clerk. "Do you have a bathroom?"

"Uh, yeah?" he replied with a grimace since even he knew how nasty the bathrooms were. It was the clerks job to clean it but they didn't pay enough to actually do it. He handed her the key attached to a large tag like a hall pass.

"Thanks..." she said and twisted in the direction he pointed. Sinclair caught a whiff of what was to come through the door. It only got worse when she twisted the key and opened the door. The aroma of shit/piss/pussy/blood/STDs/menthol and crack smoke karate kicked her in her nostrils. The smell knocked her back a few feet and she rushed back up front to throw the keys back at the clerk.

"Are you ok mom?" Carey asked when his mother came rushing back out. She was still twisting like a child who had to pee. She ignored him and rushed around to the back of the building. He followed but turned away when she pulled down her pants and squatted. "Mother!"

He took the opportunity to program the phone so he could check on his social media accounts. Sinclair returned before he could login but it was just a matter of time until he did.

"STILL NOT TALKING TO ME?" Johnson asked when Latisha entered the office. She lifted her chin and marched by him for a reply. "Guess that's a no?"

"Actually, it's a hell naw!" she stopped and popped. "I can't believe you were going to let the kid wag on a murder just because you're fucking the mother!"

"Man-man was a fucking death dealing dope boy! The Rollins kid did us a favor!" he shot back. The raised voices lifted heads from desk so he lowered the volume. "Don't forget you're nor squeaky clean either."

"The few bucks we get don't add up to a fucking body. Why not close the case?" she growled back. "Why would you warn her we were coming?"

"To be honest..." Johnson said and moved in even closer. "That pussy was just that good. Best I ever had."

"Probably not better than yours," she snarled and walked off. She took his statement of her dirt as a threat. It was the only reason she didn't report what he did. They still had a major case to solve so she turned her attention to the tourist murder.

Meanwhile, Johnson went back to searching for the fugitive mother and son. Only because he wanted to fuck the mother. He could give a fuck about the son. The phones led nowhere so he had nowhere to start. Sinclair didn't have any social media accounts so that was a dead end. His lips twisted as he tried to recall the son's nickname.

"C-block, C-murder…" he said and tried those names. His fingers snapped when it came to him. "C-note!"

It took some surfing and searching until he found the right one. He recognized Carey and checked his last post. It was dated a few days ago but he now had a lead. If C-note showed his face he would be waiting. Luckily Carey junior was a dumb ass so he wouldn't have to wait long.

CHAPTER TWELVE

Sinclair was professional enough to rent a room without identification to stay off the radar. Not that it mattered since her son logged into his account the first chance he got.

'Sup San Antonio! Who got the weed' Carey posted in a group he found when they stopped in the city for rest. A few seconds later his inbox buzzed with the knuckle heads who sold weed to strangers via social media. It was good money but high risk for both the seller and the buyer.

"I'm going for food," Carey said as casually as he would when they weren't on the run.

"Food?" she had to ask. Sinclair knew what the word meant, it just didn't go with their circumstances. One because they had just eaten more burgers in the car plus the fact that they were on the run. To make matters worse he had his hand out for money since he was broke.

"Weed if you really want to know! I need weed! You're the one who has us out here sleeping in the car and fleabag motels!" the ungrateful brat fussed. They had made it over a week already by sleeping in the car and fleabag motels.

"You know what..." she began, then folded like she always did. She could have told him he would now be in the dangerous Fulton county jail instead of a safe motel but that would just prolong it. She dug into her purse and peeled off another hundred dollar bill.

"The hell am I supposed to get with that?" he asked scornfully and didn't reach for it. The weed man wanted five hundred for an ounce which was a pretty good deal judging by the colorful picture he sent in the inbox.

"Last time! No more!" Sinclair insisted as she added four more hundred dollar bills. Between the room, gas, food and now weed she had spent nearly a grand for the day. The money wouldn't last a week at this rate. Carey might not last that long if he wasn't careful.

Sinclair stripped out of her clothes as soon as her son left the room. By the time he reached the car she was under the hot spray of water. She tried to wriggle the showerhead off to release some tension but it was fixed in place. A deep sigh escaped at having to do it the old fashioned way. It would have been nice to be bent over with Johnson and his Johnson banging her back out but it wasn't to be. Instead she cupped her box and massaged until her knees buckled.

"Whew!" Sinclair declared as the tension lessened instantly. She washed up, dried off and claimed one of the twin beds. She was fast asleep by the time Carey reached his destination.

"You C-note?" A dred head asked when Carey arrived at the taco joint they were supposed to meet. He had already scoured through his social media page and ascertained he was a spoiled rich kid.

"Yeah!" he replied eagerly and looked around. "You must be B-5?"

"I'm is. You got the money?" the dealer asked. Now it was his turn to look around. The taco stand had a nice line so they gravitated around the side.

"You got the weed?" Carey asked as he produced the cash. B-5 turned his head causing Carey to look as well. Nothing was coming from that way since it was just a distraction. When he turned back he just caught the blur of the fist speeding towards his chin. The crack of the blow echoed in the thin night air but he didn't hear it since he was sound asleep.

"Don't buy weed from strangers online," B-5 laughed as he took the money from his hand. He walked off with a chuckle and blocked him from his social media. Now he had enough to buy some weed for himself, hit the club and get something to eat.

"OWWWW," Carey moaned as he awoke a few minutes later.

"You ok?" a Mexican man asked from a nearby table where he was eating his tacos. He watched the knockout from the line, then watched the sleeping man as he ate.

"I...owww!" he began but realized his jaw was broken when he tried to open his mouth.

"Yeah, you got clocked pretty good. Want a taco?" he offered if it would help.

"I-think-my-jaw-is-broken?" he mumbled through clenched teeth.

"Probably," he agreed and looked around. The coast wasn't clear but he still went into his pocket and came out with a packet of brownish powder. He scooped some out with a fingernail as he came over. "Here, this will help."

Carey leaned in and inhaled, since it would help and all. And help it did almost instantly. A warm euphoria swept through his body and took the pain away. "What is..."

"This?" the Mexican laughed as he finished his question as Carey's head dropped to his chest in a deep nod. "That Mexican mud homie."

The man enjoyed his food while Carey enjoyed the high of his life. A smile spread on his face even while he was nodding. He was still smiling when he finally came back around.

"I feel..." Carey began and paused to find the right word.

"Good?" his new companion asked. Carey squinted at the man to see where he knew him from but couldn't recall much before the knockout.

"Great actually!" he said and wiggled his jaw. It was still just as broken but didn't hurt as bad. "What was that?"

"You never had perc or oxy?" he asked for an answer. Carey's head nodded and he continued. "Well this is their granddaddy!"

"Got more?" Carey asked since his drug of choice had just changed.

"Sure. Can you get more money?" he answered and asked. He knew the answer since Carey looked like money.

"Uh, yeah," he said and felt for the car keys. "Will you be here?"

"Of course!" the man agreed since this was his spot to move heroin. Carey rushed off to head back to the hotel to get more money while he took the opportunity to cut the dope even further. He could have sold him less for more but wanted to do the kid a favor since he would most likely kill himself with his nearly pure product.

CAREY LIFTED his heavy head after another deep nod. His eyes tried to adjust to the scenery speeding by the window in a blur. His head was still heavy so he shifted his eyes to see his stoic mother behind the wheel. He heard her suck her teeth and remembered getting chewed out.

"You're still mad at me mother?" Carey asked as she stared straight ahead. The constant use of heroin kept the pain of his broken jaw to a dull ache.

"Why would I possibly be mad at you?" she quipped sarcastically. It was a question but she didn't wait for an answer. "Because you took a thousand dollars from my purse while I slept? Because you're using god knows what drug that keeps you nodding off? No, wait! Mad because you bought a phone that can give us away?"

"Where are we?" he asked instead of answering any of her rhetorical questions. The scenery was beautiful yet foreign.

"Mexico," she replied and cast a side eye glance. Her destination was Belize where she planned to lay low. Not as low as she would like since her son took money from her purse. His jaw was swollen and purple from the blow. "I'm taking you to a doctor."

"I don't... owww!" he tried to reply but a sharp pain made it a lie before he could get it out. He gave up the protest and leaned back into his seat. They spent a few nights in a few hotels along the long drive through the country before reaching Belize.

The medical system in Belize was cheaper than the states but set her back a few hundred. Having his jaw wired shut didn't stop him from moaning and complaining about everything. Especially the liquid diet he would be on until he healed.

"I'm-fucking-hungry!" Carey griped through the wire and pouted.

"Have another shake," Sinclair suggested and reached for the protein shakes she bought to keep him full. The car swerved since she was driving and catering for her spoiled child.

"Tired-of-fucking-shakes!" he fusses but took it anyway. He was really irritable about her not stopping so he could sneak a hit of heroin. But Sinclair vowed not to stop again until they reached their hotel in Belize city. Her husband had taken her to the lower priced spot away from the tourist area many years ago. Before he got wealthy enough for the five star hotels they were accustomed to.

It was perfect now since he didn't have much money left. And perfect since they were on the run. They couldn't take a chance at being spotted by someone vacationing from Atlanta. Especially since Carey and his mother were still the top story back in the city.

'STILL NO SIGNS of the suburban housewife and her wanted son. It's been weeks since Carey Rollins cut his ankle monitor and skipped bail. Police say his mother Sinclair Rollins helped him escape and a warrant has been issued for aiding and abetting a fugitive...'

"I don't know how they managed to evade capture this long?" Carey senior wondered with Marquita laying on his chest.

"Hmp!" she huffed since she had a personal stake in their capture. It burned her up that Carey junior would have gotten away with killing her son if not for the Atlanta murder of Man-man.

"I know babe," he comforted and kissed the top of her head. She looked up so he planted one on her forehead.

"Here too," she requested and turned her cheek. He kissed there too so she puckered her lips and got a kiss there too. A mischievous grin formed on her face as she rolled off and onto her back. She lifted her sleep T-shirt and made another request. "Here too..."

"That's probably going to need more than a kiss," he suggested and kissed his way down. He didn't mind providing whatever it needed since it was his happy place. The house was their happy place where they met every day after work.

Carey tried not to look at his own house when he came and left. It grew further out of his reach with each day that passed. Pride prevented him from talking to Duane again since he benefited from his wife's deception. He consulted with another attorney who confirmed the house would be forfeited. His only option would be to be first on the courthouse steps when it was sold at auction. His head shook again at the thought of paying for the house a second time.

"Mm-mm," Marquita moaned, since shaking his head

with his tongue in her box was a good look. A good lick too so he did it again.

Marquita pulled him up face to face once he had worked up and whipped up a good froth. She happily licked the juice from his lips as he worked himself inside of her. They made sure they made love everyday since finally getting together. They increased to twice a day since her period should be near.

"Sheesh!" he exclaimed when he was snugly inside of her. She stifled a giggle at his amazement each time he entered her. Some pussy is just amazing like that. Hers was some pussy.

"I know right!" she giggled and gave him a squeeze. He stifled her giggles with his tongue and found his stroke. They were now sexually in sync and knew just how to move to make the other moan and groan. Hum and come.

They managed to find peace even in their tragedies. A balance of pain and pleasure, loss and gain that could last forever or come crumbling down at any moment. Not this moment though because they were on the verge of their nightly mutual climax.

Life was good but would it last?

CHAPTER THIRTEEN

"Really?" Sinclair wondered as her son nodded in the hotel room. He seemed antsy when they reached the hotel and rushed straight into the bathroom. Only to come out with a goofy grin and nod off on his bed. A good mother would have searched his belongings and found the cause of his recent changes. Sinclair was no good mother which was why they were on the lam and in a hotel in Belize.

"Hmp!" she huffed when she counted her money. Her head shook at what was left, then shook some more at how much her son spent.

Life on the run isn't sustainable at the rate they were burning through their cash. The prudent thing would be to shut down and be more conservative. Sinclair was as prudent as she was a good mother, meaning not at all. She showered, changed and slipped into a cute sundress she bought along the way. She counted out a couple hundred dollars and put the rest in the room safe.

The low thud of bass pulled her to the left when she

stepped out into the muggy night air. A gentle breeze swept through like a whisper but didn't provide any relief. Sinclair was in search of relief so she followed her ears as the music got louder. Then came the laughter and voices of people having a good time.

The touristy clubs offered watered down reggae to go with their watered down drinks. This was the spot where the locals came to party. Weed smoke hung in the air like fog in an eighties rock video. The floor was slightly sticky from the inevitable spilled drinks that come with a good time.

Sinclair made her way over to the bar and looked down at the menu. She wasn't in the mood for some fruity concoction with multiple colors and mini umbrellas. No, wanted something that packed a punch since she was trying to get fucked up. The woman next to her looked fairly tipsy with her eyes closed as she swayed to the music. That was exactly where she needed to be so she summoned the barkeep.

"I'll have what she's having," she requested and pointed at the woman on the next barstool.

"Rum punch," she nodded and turned to fix one up. The name had more to do with the effects of all that rum than the scant amount of fruit juice in the drink. The woman gave a wide berth to the lit candle when she delivered it since the drink was highly flammable.

"Thank you. I'll need another one soon," Sinclair said as she pulled out her money to pay for the drink.

"Yeah, no you won't," the woman laughed. The woman on the other barstool proved her right when she tipped over and fell on the floor below.

"Or not," Sinclair chuckled and took a sip. Another sip

followed by a swallow, then a gulp. It wasn't long until she felt the warm glow of inebriation sweep through her.

"Whata gwan?" a tall, dark, young dred head asked.

"Excuse me?" Sinclair asked in confusion. She put the words together fairly quickly but it was he that confused her. The her in her panties that throbbed with the beat of the bass booming through the speakers. Sweat gave his smooth, dark skin a sheen that framed his bright smile.

"Robert," he said so she knew who was pulling her onto the dancefloor.

"Sin, Sin, Sin-something?" she slurred as he pulled her into his muscular body. "Mmmm."

Robert usually worked the tourist at the touristy clubs but took a night off to enjoy some authentic music, food and drink. Still he couldn't pass on the Yankee woman at the bar when he saw her pull out that wad of Yankee cash. Especially after seeing her gulping down the rum punch that packed a sucker punch. Timing was everything once she reached the bottom of the glass.

"You 'ave a 'usband?" he asked as he gripped her ass and grinded his erection against her torso since he was so much taller than her.

"No!" she shot back, then remembered the son she left nodding back in the room. "My son is in the room."

"Wanna walk 'pon the beach?" he offered since his wife and kids were at his house. His wife didn't mind him hustling the tourist which kinda made her his pimp. She drew the line at bringing them home though.

"Ok," Sinclair agreed even though she was walking sideways from the liquor. No worries since Robert scooped her under his muscular arm and led her away. Robert walked her down to the beach and away from the bars. He didn't have a blanket so he pulled his shirt over his head and laid it down.

"Yummy!" Sinclair cheered and clapped when she peeped his pecs and abs. His rippled torso glistened in the moon light and she needed a taste.

"Yah mon," he agreed when she sucked his nipples and licked his square pectoral muscles. She worked her way down and kissed his six pack of abs. Robert whipped out the dick and handed it over like an offering. She eagerly accepted it as far down her throat as she could take. "Yah mon!"

'Gawk' she replied when the tip touched her tonsils. She wanted to keep going but Robert had other ideas. She was a far cry from the overweight and out of shape tourist who usually paid him for sex. She was pretty, shapely and clean so he laid her down and dipped under her sundress.

"Oh!" Sinclair gasped when he snatched her panties aside and clamped his whole mouth over her whole box. She squirmed as he sucked her like a ripe mango. Once she got juicy like a mango he rushed up and stuffed her full of dick.

Sinclair grabbed handfuls of sand as he lifted her legs under his elbows. All she could do was hold on while he pile drove the dick all up him her guts. The stars above began to twirl so she closed her eyes and held on. The last thing she remembered was busting a nut and howling in the night air.

"Good night miss Sin-something," Robert laughed when her head lolled to the side. She began to snore lightly but that didn't stop his stroke. She had some good gushy pussy so he didn't let it go to waste. He reached under her and grabbed her ass cheeks and dug her out real good. She didn't object when he finally exploded inside of her. "Yah mon!"

Sinclair dreamt a wonderful dream about a handsome young man with long dreds and a thick dick. They danced, laughed and made love under the moonlight. The combination of the rising sun and voices pulled her from the peaceful slumber.

"Huh?" she asked up at the blue sky when her eyes opened. She sat up and looked around to gain her bearings. The throb of her vagina told her the thick dick was no dream but there was no dred in sight. Nor her purse containing her money. Robert didn't fuck for free so he took his fee. His wife would enjoy the purse and trinkets inside. "Awe man!"

"WHERE THE HELL HAVE YOU BEEN!" Carey junior barked when his mother walked in.

"Out! And I'm not in the mood for your mouth right now!" Sinclair fussed on her way into the bathroom. Not only had she been fucked and ducked but her ass was full of sand and semen at the moment. All she wanted was a cool shower and put some food on her growling belly.

"I wanted breakfast but don't have money," Carey tried again a little softer when his mother returned from rinsing Roberts residue from inside of her. He thought she may have kept it in her purse but couldn't find it either while she showered. Mainly because Robert's wife was putting her stuff in it right now.

"We can go to breakfast, but," she sighed and paused. "We're going to need more money. And soon."

"Yeah," he agreed since he needed more heroin soon.

The mother and son headed down to the restaurant and ate in silence. Both were consumed with their thoughts of how to get more money. Plus Carey needed to have fun and party. Being on the run was no fun since they had just been driving for days. Mama went out and got laid now he was ready to have some fun.

"Give me your phone," Sinclair demanded across the table. Carey huffed and puffed in protest but came off it. He watched the men in the restaurant watch his mother as she stepped aside to make a call. His mother was his mother so he couldn't identify just how fine she was. When he turned away he saw a pretty girl staring in his direction. Carey tried to crack a smile that reminded him of his broken jaw. The resulting wince brought the young woman over.

"Am I that ugly?" she dared and laughed as she stood over him. Carey locked in on her bare navel in the midriff shirt and forgot the question. She was nearly as light as his mother but shorter and thicker.

"Huh?" he asked when she laughed at his confusion.

"Anyway, I'm Carol. I'm here with my parents," she said and nodded towards the handsome couple a few tables away. Her pretty mother kept an eye on her while her handsome father's eyes roamed the room. They scanned every breast and ass in sight,

"Carey. That's my mom," he managed and nodded towards Sinclair.

"Are you ok?" Carol asked when she saw he was clearly in pain. His head began to nod but she turned and called for her father. "Dad!"

"Yes Carol?" he replied as he came over with his wife in

tow. He responded to her but was looking at him. His wayward daughter had been through a lot lately so he came rushing over.

"My friend Carey is hurt," she said and the doctor immediately noticed the contusion on his jaw.

"Your jaw is probably broken," he guessed. Carey confirmed the guess when he replied through semi clenched teeth.

"I'm fine. I just fell," he said to the doctor's shaking head.

"See, if you guys hadn't taken all of my oxi I could help!" Carol protested and stomped her foot like the spoiled brat she was. Her parents brought her down here as a bribe before going to rehab to shake her budding opiate addiction.

"Now Carol..." her mother cooed before the brat stomped away. Her mother followed behind begging for her to talk.

"Is everything ok?" Sinclair asked as she came back. She didn't get to make her call since she saw her son talking to fellow Americans. She accepted he wasn't smart enough not to give his real name and give them away.

"No, his jaw is broken. He needs to have it set properly," he assured since he could tell it wasn't done correctly. Sinclair watched his eyes dip to her chest and find a smile when they returned to her face. They had a moment before her brat spoke up.

"Excuse me! My jaw?" he interrupted. But not before a connection was made between the cheating husband and wayward wife.

"Yes, we're headed to our family doctor once we return to the states!" she assured and pulled Carey up by his arm.

"Are you guys staying in the hotel?" he asked to see if he would see her later.

"We are," she nodded to the question he asked as well as the one he didn't. "Sinclair."

"Rafael," he said and gave her his hand. They locked eyes and made tacit plans to hook up before she walked away. He bit his lip as he watched her round ass shift away.

CHAPTER FOURTEEN

"I'm going out. Can I have my phone and some money?" Carey asked through his newly wired jaw. He had a fresh hit of heroin to numb the pain. Then took a hot shower after coming out of his nod. A bellhop said he could get him some good dope but now he needed some money to pay for it.

"Ok to going out. No to the phone and just a few dollars. We have to conserve!" she reminded and parted with a hundred dollar bill. "Make it last!"

"It's a hundred tho?" he asked incredulously. He used to spend that much on lunch in his old life and hadn't adjusted to his new life.

"Mmhm," Sinclair hummed since she really wasn't listening. She was primping and preparing for her own rendezvous and didn't have time for him.

Plus she still needed to get some money from somewhere. The door closing alerted her that her son had left the room. He quickly caught up with the bellhop and copped what he could for the hundred. Carey had spotted Carol by the pool and headed down to meet her. She was sulking with her feet in the water when he came up behind her.

"Don't jump!" he said playfully and gave her a slight push.

"I may as well jump off a building!" she fussed and fell forward into the pool. Carey watched curiously as she sank lifelessly to the bottom. He debated on if he should go in after her or walk away. He was just about to walk off when she kicked off the bottom of the pool and swam back up. Evidently the water refreshed her spirits since she was smiling when she emerged from the water.

"What the hell?" he wondered of the incident. "Who swims with all their clothes on!"

"People with no life! My parents are killing me slowly!" she moaned as he helped her from the water. Her thin T-shirt and shorts had practically dissolved and showed her fine frame in all its yellow glory.

"Shit you're fine!" he blurted before he could stop himself. Good thing he didn't, since she smiled and blushed at the compliment. "How old are you?"

"Thanks," she cooed and ducked coyly. It was refreshing to see but he still wanted to corrupt her. She ducked the question about her age since he wouldn't like the answer.

"What were you talking about earlier? About Oxi?" he asked. Her eyes went wide and lit up at the mention of her favorite drug.

"You got some!" she demanded and nearly patted his pockets.

"Um, no," he said and watched her face go sad again. He knew he had gotten in over his head with his new drug but hated to see her sad. Plus her clothes were still stuck to her body and he wanted to fuck her. "I have something better. Where can we go?"

"Uh, we're at a beach resort. We can go to the beach, duh!" she teased. Her happiness overcame his reservation's so off they went. She filled him in about her deprived life back in Rhode Island with her doctor dad and manager mom.

Her upper class life was spoiled by her protective parents trying to keep her off drugs. A lot of kids experiment with drugs in high school. Most use it as a passing phase and move on with life. Some get stuck with lifelong habits, Carol was some. She had gotten into her mom's oxycontin supply and never let up. Once her parents got wind of it they booked her into a rehab facility. They decided to take her to the Central American country to wait for the next bed to come available.

"Oh my God! I've been doing all the talking!" Carol gushed as they came to a stop. They sank to the sand a few feet from where Carey's mother's ass print was left from the night before. "Tell me about you?"

"Not much to tell.." he said and paused. There really wasn't much he could say since he was actually a double murderer on the run. So he pulled the package and changed the subject. "Have you ever tried this?"

"Sure!" she lied and reached for it. "What is it!"

"Super Oxy!" he said since it sounded sexier than the truth. Even he didn't like the sound of heroin.

"Give me some!" she demanded like brats demand things. Except he wasn't one of her enabling parents and wanted something in return.

"I was just thinking the same thing!" he said and reached for her breast. Carol smiled and looked down to watch him fondle her through the wet shirt. Then watched as he pulled the shirt above her titties and kissed them. She let out a moan when he reached between her legs. She let him rub crotch until he tried to pull her panties aside.

"What?" he asked when she forcefully grabbed his wrist.

"I'm a..." she began and got stuck on the word. "I've never, I still..."

"A virgin?" he reeled since they were rare. Kelondra was one of the few he knew of before she gave it to Marquis. His face twisted into a snarl at the thought. A crooked smile from the wires soon followed at the memory of killing Marquis over it. Some people speculated he did it over losing his spot on the court but the truth was even more sinister. Hearing Kelondra had given her virginity to Marquis was more than he could bear.

"Hello?" Carol called and waved a hand in front of his face to bring him back from wherever he just went. "And yes, I'm a virgin."

"Well, how long do you plan on staying one..." he asked and leaned down to kiss her thigh. He ran his tongue up and down and back up again.

"Doesn't look like very long," she hissed when he pulled her panties aside for a lick. There wasn't enough room to really get to it so she lifted her hips to allow him to remove her shorts and panties in one pull. Another hissed filled the muggy night air.

Carol writhed in the sand as Carey ate her brand new box. She squealed a few minutes later when she climaxed in his mouth. Then watched him as he climbed between her legs. She winced when he squeezed inside of her and slowly pumped. There wouldn't be too many pumps in the tight space before he couldn't take any more.

"Shit!" Carey shouted and slumped over on top of her.

"Um, I'm pretty sure you should get up?" the girl guessed since he hadn't used protection. But mainly because she was ready to try the super oxy. Oxy made her feel super enough as it were so she was ready to try this super version of his.

"My bad," he agreed and withdrew the dick. The wet sheen was tinged from her blood and he added another body to his list. He had deflowered more girls than he could count.

"No worries! Now can we try the stuff?" she wondered. "I have to go to rehab Tuesday so I may as well have some fun."

"Rehab sucks!" he recalled since several of his friends back in West View had been. He pulled the package back out and showed her how to take a hit up each nostril. Once he was done he passed it to her. She did what he did but doubled up in each nostril. "Take it easy!"

"I'll be in rehab Tuesday! May as well live it up!" she cheered. The cheer died soon after when both of their heads got heavy all of a sudden. Soon they were both in a deep nod as the drug coursed through their young bodies.

"I'M GOING to head out for a few. For a drink," Rafael said as he checked himself in the mirror.

"I'm sure," his wife said and twisted her lips. She saw all the pretty women around the hotel and knew her husband well enough to know he was going to meet with one of them. Maybe two since she knew him that well. She wasn't a selfish wife like Sinclair, her husband just wanted more pussy than she had. She only had one, a pretty good one but her husband needed more than one. "Send your daughter back up to the room if you see her."

"If I see her," he said over his shoulder as he left the room. He smoothed his shirt and inhaled the Killa cologne he was wearing. The scent was named after the mythical murderer from the Bronx and ladies loved it.

Rafael had made a few connections while out with his wife and daughter. Now he was ready to consummate one since he didn't have his wife and daughter now. His destination was the pool so he looked around for his daughter. The first glance didn't produce her so he looked around and saw Sinclair looking back. The doctor cracked a smile and headed over.

"Well hello there doctor Rafael!" Sinclair greeted as he approached. He kept coming until he invaded her space and gave her a hug. "Oh, ok?"

"How's your son?" he wondered since he was a doctor and all. The pursuit of pussy didn't deter him from his Hippocratic oath.

"You were right. I called his doctor back home. We'll take him when we return," she sighed. Not just over the injury but the doctor took another chunk of her money not to have done it right. She sighed and tossed the rest of her drink back. After thirty minutes of waiting she had a pretty good buzz going.

"Let me buy you another?" he offered and waved the bartender over. The woman came over and twisted her lips at the married man. She served him and his family by day only to serve him and some other woman each night. "Bring her another please."

"Mmhm," the woman said and mixed another apple martini. It would be her third but three more came after that.

"I assume that woman was your wife? And she's in the room?" Sinclair slurred when she was ready to go.

"You would be correct," he replied. He may cheat but didn't lie about it. "And I assume your son would be resting in your room?"

"We can go to the beach!" she suggested since she had just gotten laid on the beach the night before. He agreed by taking her by the elbow and helping her out. Neither looked back so they didn't see the doctor's wife watching from the balcony. She had been looking for Carol and just happened to catch a glimpse of her husband and his latest conquest.

"Easy!" Rafael chuckled when Sinclair stumbled since she was stumbling drunk. He scanned the darkened beach for a good spot to lay her down. It seemed like everyone had the same idea since copulating couples dotted the treeline. Soft moans and guttural groans filled the night as they walked along.

"That's how I want it," Sinclair suggested as they passed a woman riding a man on a blanket.

"And that's how you shall..." Rafael was saying until a familiar sight stopped him in his tracks. His daughter's bright orange top was clearly visible even in the moonlight. His eyes squinted in scrutiny as he approached. They walked up on the two half naked teens sprawled out in the sand.

"Carey!" Sinclair shouted down at her son while the doctor called for his daughter. "Carol!"

Neither moved so he flipped her over and saw the foam coming from her mouth and the faraway look of death in her arms. Both had ODd but Carey was unlucky enough to live.

The wounded doctor's howls brought attention that brought authorities. Soon the beach was crawling with Belizian police.

The Rollins run on the run had run its course when the cops came. The drugs in his pocket was enough to get him arrested but when his fingerprints were entered into Interpol the warrants for him popped up.

CHAPTER FIFTEEN

"What now?" Carey senior groaned when he saw the name on his screen. Lately anyone from his old life only came with bad news. The woman laying next to him represented his new life and life was good. He may have lost a half million dollar house but he was happy and that shit is priceless.

"What's wrong babe?" Marquita asked as she popped up. The hood chick in her had her ready to handle whatever was wrong. If he was hungry she would make a sandwich. If his dick was hard she would ride it until it got soft again.

"The lawyer..." he sighed and took the call. He assumed it wasn't good news and was right.

"Sorry to call so late but..." Duane lied. He didn't mind at all since he was just snatched from his sleep by an international call.

"They found them," Carey guessed since he couldn't think of any other reason for the call. He hit the speaker so Marquita could hear as well.

"In Belize. Carey gave a fifteen year old girl drugs. She

died," he reported and paused for a reply. None came so he asked, "You there? Did you hear me?"

"Uh, yeah. I'm just not sure why you would call me?" Carey strained to understand.

"Well, I'm going to need a lot of money to take these charges! I..." Duane was saying until his screen saver popped on his screen. "Hello? This nigga done hung up on me?"

"Wow!" Marquita reeled and winced at the bad news. The boy just seemed to be cursed to cause destruction everywhere he went. They both sat in silence as if trying to figure it out.

"I'm trying to think, trying to remember how, when, where..." Carey strained and thought. "Something, somewhere went wrong?"

"Un-uh! That's what we not doing!" she fussed and turned his face by his chin like a mother does a truculent child. "You're a good man! This ain't none of your fault! That sorry ass wife of yours messed that boy up!"

"You're right about that. She never disciplined him. Just let him do whatever he wanted to do," he reflected.

"Well, you don't seem too happy they got caught," Marquita dared.

"Happy?" Carey asked and searched for his feelings. He wasn't happy but by no means was he sad either. "I mean, if my son got the death penalty for killing your son, that would be justice. Perfectly fair, exactly what he deserves. But that wouldn't make me happy. There is no happiness for me. I love you and I hate that we lost your son."

"Yeah," she sighed as the words made sense. He was caught in the middle of the worst possible scenario. Plus she had another pressing matter and wondered if this was the right time to share it.

"What?" Carey asked when he saw her drift away into her head.

"I'm just saying. We both lost our only child," she said and paused at the grim reality. Carey junior would have gotten a slap on the wrist for killing her son but he was dead on Man-man's murder. Then the feds were going to charge him with the death of a United States citizen abroad. That carried a possible death penalty. "We're gonna have to do a better job with this next one."

"Next what? What do you mean?" he asked, matching her mischievous smile.

"I mean all 'dat, 'argh, shit, I'm coming'," she mimicked and made the faces Carey made when he climaxed. "All in me, err night!"

"Are you saying..." he reeled and looked at her hard stomach.

"That you finna be a daddy," she revealed. Marquita tried to keep a straight face until she saw his reaction but she was too happy not to smile.

"Wow," he said and stared straight ahead. Marquita's smile began to dissipate when she saw the stoic look on his face. It had all but vanished before the corner of his mouth began to turn up. It continued until he wore the straight, bright smile she loved so much. Carey was one of those calculated people who thought before they spoke. "That's great. Fantastic!"

"So, you're happy?" she asked even though they were both cheesing like Cheshire cats.

"Ecstatic!" he cheered and kissed her all over her face.

"A'ight now, this is how you got us in this position!" Marquita warned and mocked his fuck face again. 'Argh, I'm coming!'

"I know ms, 'ooh, I'm finna come!' isn't talking smack!" he dared. The laughter led to a kiss, a lick and a full fledged session of making love.

"I'M NOT SURE WHAT, if anything I can do to help?" Thomas, the Belizean lawyer wondered. Sinclair came to his office seeking help before Carey could be extradited back to the states. He knew American courtrooms were bigger than the whole country so he wasn't sure what could be done, if anything.

"Are you sure you can't help us?" Sinclair purred and dropped the top of her sundress. The lawyer nodded at the nice set of breasts before him. They were actually very nice but wouldn't help him get out of this mess.

"Positive," he assured and away went the breast. "I suggest getting a lawyer in the states who can..."

"Yeah," she cut in and turned around. Duane had told her the same thing but she was too stubborn to accept it. She had already tried to seduce the officers at the station but to no avail. Carey was about to be picked up by the FBI so she decided to try her luck with the agents.

Sinclair marched over to the police station just as agents arrived. They were here to return Carey to the states to face both the state charges he was running from as well as the new federal charges he was facing for Carol's death. She didn't have much money left but planned to offer her orifices in exchange for her son.

"Excuse me, officers..." Sinclair called and struck a pose.

"Agents," one of the agents corrected while the other one squinted in disbelief. He looked into his folder and back over at Sinclair.

"Sinclair Rollins?" the agent asked hopefully. His luck was usually never this good.

"Yesssss," she hissed seductively and out came the cuffs.

"You have a warrant for aiding and abetting a fugitive..." he said as he cuffed her hands behind her back. The mother and son would be united on the flight back to the states.

"HUH?" Carey asked when he returned home to find a familiar car in the driveway. The driver never came with good news so he prepared himself as he went inside.

"Hey Carey. You remember detective Adams," Marquita announced as he walked in.

"Detective," he nodded to her and turned back to his woman. "Is everything ok?"

"Naw, not really. They got him in the Atlanta jail," she replied while the detective watched closely for his reaction. It was so slight only a detective would have detected it.

"And your wife is in the West View jail for aiding and abetting," Latisha added and watched.

"Ex, ex wife," he quickly corrected.

"Oh, I didn't know you guys divorced?" the cop questioned and watched some more. This time her eyes tilted towards Marquita to see how she felt about what was to come.

"I filed. Now that she's back she can be served," he replied towards his new woman.

"So, what now?" Marquita asked since she had never been on this side of a case.

"Well, now he goes to court. Either a trail or a plea bargain," she said and stood. Carey was a gentleman so he stood as well to walk her out. They only made it two steps before the detective had one final question of her own. This one was off the record so she didn't need to pull her pad back out. "How does this work?"

"This what?" Carey asked but Marquita understood the question.

"It just does. They find gold and diamonds in the rocks and mud don't they?" she explained.

"They do," Latisha nodded at the analogy. These two had certainly found love in the mud. The couple stayed quiet until the cop had driven away.

"Fuck she mean, how this work!" Marquita fussed and touched her stomach. She was months away from showing but just knowing a person was growing inside of her brought her hand there several times a day. Even the detective noticed it during their talk.

"It's unorthodox to say the least. Almost like some sappy urban romance book," he laughed.

"I know right!" she laughed along with him. "How 'bout, To love and die in Atlanta!"

"Nah, sounds corny!" Carey said, shaking his head. He too touched her stomach and popped a kiss on her lips before heading out to crank up the grill. Life was good, for now.

"THANK GOD YOU'RE HERE! Get me out of this place so we can get my son!" Sinclair demanded when Duane McCoy entered the attorney room to meet with his client.

"Um," he paused and searched for the right words. For the first time he realized this woman was crazy. Her privileged life had deluded her into thinking she could get out of everything. "It's not that simple. First of all, your husband won't take my calls. I'm not paid to work on your case."

"I paid you plenty!" she reminded and lifted her chin defiantly. Duane realized she was beyond reasoning so he gave in. Besides, he had taxed her far beyond reason for her son's case.

"I might be able to get you a bond, but," he said and sighed, He left the rest for her to finish but she stared ahead like a deer caught in the headlights. He knew if Carey wasn't taking his calls he certainly wouldn't be paying her bond. Especially after losing his home.

"I have to save my son," she pleaded and something squeezed in the place where his heart would be if he had one.

"No worries," he assured and stood. She reached across and touched his crotch when he did.

"No worries here either. I'll take good care of..." she tried to pur but he knocked her hand away before the guard across the room could object. He couldn't hear the privileged conversation but made sure nothing was passed during the visit. His standing was his cue to come take the prisoner back to her dorm.

"I'm married now," he reminded and showed the ring she paid for on his ringer finger.

"So I am, but that never stopped us before!" she shouted as he headed for the door. "It didn't stop us from fucking and sucking while I was married!"

"Time to go Miss Rollins," the officer said once the room was clear.

"Mrs! That's Mrs Rollins!" she fussed and pulled away from his grip. He knew these privileged rich folks were harder to deal with than the hardened inner city folks so he let her walk without the cuffs. "I think I'm going back to my husband!"

CHAPTER SIXTEEN

Carey had his hands filled when he reached the Fulton county jail. The city jail had a detox unit to process the new junkies upon arrival. After a week of sweats and shits he was taken up to the notorious eighth floor of the jail. All sound and movement stopped when the door opened. Then resumed once it closed.

"What do they call you?" a teen asked as he sized up the new face in the dorm. This dorm was used to house the city's killers until they made bond or went to trial. It was filled with dangerous dope boys and gang bangers who chose violence over reason. It looked like a convention of baby face murderers since no one over twenty one.

"C-note!" Carey said and tilted his head like a dare. That was the easy question, it was the next one that mattered most.

"What you bang?" he asked and all talk stopped. The staff usually tried to balance the amount of each gang to keep the fights fair.

"West view Vikings!" Carey junior shot back and puffed

his chest. The name held a little weight in the suburbs and the suburban mall but meant nothing in this land of Riders and Rollers.

"Who? What? The fuck?" the bangers around the room wondered and looked around to see who got to claim him. Some obscure gangs are loosely affiliated with bigger gangs but no one heard of them. Someone heard of C-note though.

"Ooh! Ooh! I know that nigga!" a voice called out from the Riders side. All eyes turned to the speaker who spoke up as he came forward. "Yeah, that's you!"

"Sup Scooter!" Carey replied, almost happy to see a familiar face. It only took a second to recall why he was here and he wasn't happy to see him anymore. "That's fucked up you killed my partner!"

"I ain't kill that nigga! I just robbed him!" Scooter shot back and shrugged. He glanced around and pointed to one of the Rollers. "He's the one shot yo people!"

"Shole did! You want some smoke about it?" Ray-ray dared. He and Bay-bay were kept in separate housing units since they were both testifying against one another.

"Nah, I'm good. I don't want no smoke about nothing," Carey admitted. The thing about that is you can't walk into a forest fire and claim not to want smoke. The gang infested jail was on fire and he was about to die from smoke inhalation or one of them homemade knives.

"I was in court with that nigga! He the one kilt Man-man!" another teen shouted. That revelation set off more murmurs and threats. Man-man was well liked and respected in the city.

"Rollins! Attorney visit!" the officer called as he entered the dorm just before Carey got it from all sides. Oddly enough these dangerous men folded up like napkins when the police came in. Most were straight terrors in the hood but not a one put up a fight when the cops came to take them away forever.

"Yes!" Carey shouted and ran over to the officer before he got attacked. He followed him away but knew he had to come back and face the music. The guard escorted him into a small booth with thick glass in between.

"Hey Carey I just..." Duane was saying until Carey pleaded for his life.

"You gotta get me out of here! These people are going to kill me!" he shouted through the bullet proof partition that separated them. Duane just sighed and shook his head. It still hadn't dawned on him and his mother just how much trouble he was in. He took a deep breath and gave it to him as plainly as possible.

"Carey, you're going to die in jail. If they don't kill you old age will," he stated and let that sink in before proceeding. Both the Feds and Fulton county wanted a life sentence even if West view was still willing to sweep Marquis's death under the rug.

"But, but, but..." he protested but the lawyer had a rebuttal for every but. He wasn't quite as naive as his mother and accepted his fate. The best he could hope for was to serve his time in the federal system instead of the notoriously dangerous Georgia state prison system. "What about my mom?"

"Plead to involuntary manslaughter in West view and she'll get probation," he advised. Her bond was secured by the ten percent he put down and she was being processed out as they spoke. Sinclair didn't have a good track record but he had bilked her out of enough money to absorb the loss if necessary.

"Ok," Carey said and prepared to face his fate. There's a calmness that comes from accepting one's fate even if it means death. Except he was just as much a killer as any of those kids in his dorm. He cuffed the pen used to sign off on the West view plea deal that would spare his mother.

"Be safe," Duane said as they stood and parted through opposite doors.

"Yeah, I'll be safe. They need to be safe from me," he grumbled as the officer took him back to the dorm. This time he marched ahead instead of lagging behind.

Once again the activity and speech came to an abrupt end when the door slid open. The entire dorm made the decision to pop it off on Carey when he returned. Scooter got the honor of setting it off so he lingered near the door to attack as soon as it closed.

Except Carey didn't play by their rules. As soon as the officer removed one of his cuffs he rushed over and drove the pen into his eye. The sudden violence caught even the officer off guard. Carey used the steel handcuffs to attack Ray-ray next. Each blow opened a deep gash on his face and head.

"Everybody down!" the officer shouted before pulling his taser. Everyone complied except for Carey until fifty thousand volts made him go stiff.

The extreme violence certainly earned the inmates respect but it wouldn't be needed. Carey was deemed too dangerous for general population and put in administrative segregation. It would be his home until he went to court.

❅

"ARGH! WHEW! MMMM!" Both Carey and Marquita hummed and groaned after their nightly love making session. They had heard some thumping and banging while they were thumping and banging but assumed it was their thumping and banging so they ignored it.

"The heck is that?" Carey wondered, winded from the good sex. Marquita had already stood on wobbly legs from busting a nut so she peeped out the window.

"Um, yo wife!" she reeled and stepped aside to share the window when he rushed over. They both watched as Sinclair attempted to pull down the boards that blocked the windows and doors of the old house that used to be their home. "You better get her 'fo the cops come!"

"Why?" he wondered since he felt absolutely nothing for the woman. They say when a woman's fed up there ain't nothing you can do about but it's the same for a man. Even his warm, soft heart had grown cold towards the woman.

"Carey!" Marquita fussed when the woman began shouting through the night. The Uber driver who dropped her off pulled away since he didn't want any parts of whatever she was doing.

"Oh ok!" he sighed and pulled his pajama pants on. Marquita snatched the shirt since she claimed it for her own. Carey had to settle for a T-shirt and headed out. He crossed the grass and called, "Sinclair! What are you doing here?"

"I live here!" she shouted before registering where he was coming from. "A better question is what are you doing there! With that woman! All the trouble she caused us!"

"This bitch really is just crazy!" Marquita realized. She was ready to come out and fight until hearing that.

"Are you crazy?" Carey finally caught on himself. So

many people walk around functionally crazy until the right stress or trauma brings it to the surface. Sinclair was spoiled and privileged but didn't intend to turn her kid into a killer. She did her best to handle it all but finally imploded.

"What's crazy about going home?" she wondered and looked at him like he was crazy for asking. "Too much has happened. I just want to go home. Let's go home and make it like it used to be. Remember how it used to be? It was good! Really good!"

"Oooooh!" he reeled when he smelled the alcohol on her breath when she came closer. Carey looked around to see who brought her here so they could take her back to wherever they got her from. "How did you get here?"

"My friend Arnold, Darnell, uh Harold?" she guessed and looked around. She managed to catch the tail lights as the car pulled away from the subdivision. "Why is the house locked? Did you change the locks?"

"Oh the locks are the same. The issue is you put the house up as collateral for Carey's bond. Then took him on the run!" he shouted down at her. More porch lights came on as more neighbors came to investigate.

"What the fuck these nosey neighbors looking at!" she shouted as if she hadn't been one of the nosey neighbors not long ago. "Um, nothing to see here! Go back to bed!"

"You're causing a scene," he warned but she was too far gone from the liquor and the crazy. He just shook his head when she began verbally attacking the neighbors by name.

"Amy McGuire, the soccer mom who sucked the soccer coach's dick! Misty Mulberry with a three man rotation while her husband is at work!" It worked since the doors and windows began to close. Some after being exposed, others beat her to and retreated before getting exposed.

"I'm out..." Carey said and went back inside the house. The police arrived a few minutes later and took Sinclair to a hotel to sleep it off.

"WHY IS THERE A 'FOR SALE' sign in front of the house?" Carey wondered when he came home from work.

"I was waiting to ask you?" Marquita replied as the baby in her belly fluttered in response to the voices.

"I'll call Jim Hartwell and find get to the bottom of this," Carey said since he knew the booster who owned the house. It was a perk for getting Marquis out here to play but he wasn't playing anymore.

"Carey Rollins!" Jim boomed when he took the call. He had always been fond of the man but even more so now.

"Yes, hey Jim. I saw the house across the street from me is for sale?" he asked without letting on that he lived there as well.

"Yes, it's time to unload it," he admitted and sighed before suddenly remembering. "Sucks what happened to your house but I'll give you a deal if you want? Three hundred for you after all the money your kid made me!"

"My kid? I don't follow," Carey squinted.

"Yeah, I had key man insurance on that ghetto kid. When your kid killed him I made four million dollars!" he cheered and laughed. There was no laughter on the other end which made him ask, "You still there?"

"Um, yeah. I..." he said and strained to find words. He

looked over to Marquita looking like she was ready to put her shoes on and fight whoever had his face screwed up like that. "Did the mother get a payout?"

"Absolutely not!" he laughed and explained. "If that ghetto mama wasn't smart enough to insure her ghetto bastard, that's her problem!"

"Except it's about to become your problem!" Carey vowed and hung up the phone.

"What?" Marquita asked so she could figure out how to help. She was ready toot the booty up for some back shots since that would help them both.

"We need a lawyer," he nodded. His head shook when Duane McCoy came to mind at the mention of a lawyer. "A good lawyer!"

"Wow! Just, wow!" she reeled in disbelief when he filled her in. "These bougie folks ain't about shit!"

"No dear. They most certainly are not," he had to agree. He would know after seeing life from both sides. He knew a few more lawyers and would settle on one to go after that settlement. In the meanwhile he had a few court dates to attend.

CHAPTER SEVENTEEN

"All rise!" the bailiff announced when the judge came out of her chambers. Carey senior confidently took to his feet to hear the verdict.

Sinclair and her lawyer took to their feet from the other table and leaned in to listen. Carey didn't bother hiring a lawyer for these proceedings since it was so cut and dry. His wife had multiple affairs and was now on probation for aiding and abetting their son when he was on the run. This should be quick and easy. No muss, no fuss.

"I'm going to grant the divorce in favor of the respondent," the lady judge declared. Carey scrunched his face to recall if he was the respondent or the plaintiff. He was the latter which made the ruling that much more confusing. He didn't bring up her drinking or infidelity in the pleadings. Just irreconcilable differences so they could go their separate ways in life.

"Say what?" Carey blurted before she could finish.

"Another word out of you and I'll hold you in contempt of court!" the judge admonished and continued. "You have not demonstrated any cause to grant in your favor. If anything, you have failed to protect and maintain your family. Then, to show up in my courtroom with a pregnant girlfriend is especially egregious!"

Sinclair shot a glance back at Marquita and cracked a smile. She may have won the man but it was going to cost him. She turned back as the judge continued her ruling.

"You lost the family home so I can not award that to the respondent. You will however provide spousal support in the amount of five thousand dollars a month. As well as another vehicle and insurance..." the judge went on and on until she cost Carey almost ten thousand dollars a month.

"Damn! Cheaper to keeper!" a spectator said from the row behind Marquita.

"Naw, cheaper to kill her ass," she hissed to herself as Carey made it back over to her.

"I'd pay twice that to have her out of my life!" he shrugged. Ten grand a month was a bargain to be rid of her. Now it was time to head downtown to see how his son made out. He agreed to plead out to manslaughter for Marquis's murder in West view. It would cost ten years in prison but he was facing a life sentence in Fulton county.

Duane McCoy decided he had been paid more than enough so he took that case on the strength. He and his old friend Carey senior made eye contact when he entered the courtroom but didn't speak or nod. He did glance at a very pregnant Marquita wobbling beside him. A smirk twisted his mouth to show what he thought about that.

Sinclair walked in with her head held high, still high off the fresh win in divorce court. Plus she tossed back a few shots of vodka to celebrate. She slid into the row behind the couple so she could watch them. Marquita made it a point to rub Carey's head so she could see the glittering engagement ring on her finger. The cattiness came to a sudden end when the bailiff came out and announced the court was in session.

"All rise!" he said and all rose. The side door opened and C-note was escorted out, flanked by two burly deputies. He was shackled and in his jail uniform since no potential jurors were seated in the court. Good thing too because he looked every bit the stone cold killer.

Sinclair let out an audible gasp when she saw what was left of her baby boy. Carey junior spent the last few months in a single man cell. By the look of his body he had been working out. By the look in his eyes he had lost his mind.

"Wow," Carey senior mumbled when he saw how hard he looked. Junior cracked a quarter of a smile and nodded towards his mother. He refused to look at his father or Marquita and took a seat next to his attorney.

"I understand a plea has been made?" the judge asked after looking over his notes.

"Yes, your honor. Yes sir," both sides said as they stood. Both the prosecutor and defense attorney nodded for the other to go first.

"My client has agreed to plead guilty to one count of manslaughter," Duane began and turned to the prosecutor.

"To serve twenty years since the defendant has a federal case waiting as well. He's likely to receive a life sentence which would supersede the state sentence," he explained.

"I see," the judge said and pursed his lips.

"Uh oh," Duane McCoy muttered when the judge began to frown.

"I've seen this before. The Ahmaud Arbery case. Plead

guilty in the feds to do easy time," the judge chided. His face said what he thought of that before speaking again. "He owes the state twenty years and he'll give the state twenty years. Then the feds can have him."

Carey felt Marquita involuntarily squeeze his hand. She was elated to see the young man get the worst possible sentence for taking her child away from her. Carey couldn't feel bad for someone getting what they deserved but couldn't rejoice either.

"I have to consult with my client for a..." Duane was saying but got cut off.

"No. He'll either continue his plea for twenty years, in state prison. Or take his chances with a life sentence in this court," the judge dared.

"I'll take the dub," C-note announced and tilted his head defiantly.

"You won't be safe in state prison," Duane advised. He was right too since no one was safe in state prison.

"Man I'm C-muhfuckin-note!" he declared like he believed it. He turned back to the judge and took his lick. "Guilty my nigga!"

Carey Rollins jr was sentenced to twenty years to serve in state prison. The feds would borrow him in a few months, for a few months to face that charge and be sent back to max out the twenty. Then the rest of his life would be spent in the federal penitentiary.

He looked back at his mother before being escorted back through the same door from which he came. Once again he ignored his father. The snub brought another hand squeeze from his pregnant fiance.

"Ion know why I'm sad?" Marquita wondered. She didn't feel any of the joy she thought this day would bring.

"Because there are no winners. Everyone lost," Carey said and stood. He and Sinclair locked eyes as he helped Marquita to her swollen feet. Sinclair knew she held the blame in how fucked up their kid turned out. She was too fucked up to admit it so she lifted her chin and glared.

Her husband had to foot her bills until she remarried so she planned to never remarry. Should would party, drink and fuck on his dime for the rest of her life. Carey could be all the happy he wanted to be but he would still have to take care of her.

"Oh!" Marquita announced when she and Sinclair locked eyes. "My water just broke!"

"Let's get you to the hospital!" Carey exclaimed and scooped her up. Sinclair felt a stab in her heart when she watched love in motion. She realized he was a good man and she fucked it up. Something else she would never admit so she went to get drunk.

"TAKE ME BACK TO GENERAL POPULATION," Carey advised when he reached the jail.

"I heard that," the deputy nodded. He knew what awaited and respected his decision. A quick brutal death was better than wasting away in prisons for the next fifty or sixty years, just waiting to die. Even the death penalty was a drag since the condemned would spend decades on death row waiting to die. Quite a few die of natural causes while waiting for the state sponsored murder.

Carey planned to go out fighting once he went back into the same dorm he came from. The dorm went silent when the doors opened. Eyes blinked and did double takes when they saw who it was. Carey flexed his muscles as he was uncuffed. He tensed for battle once the officer left and the door closed behind him.

Then something unexpected happened. The dorm went right back to what they were doing and saying before he came in. Carey squinted around curiously but no one paid him any attention. Scooter looked over with the one eye he had left but quickly turned away. Ray-ray ducked under his gaze as well and retreated to his cell.

"Thought y'all wanted some smoke!" Carey dared. He was ready to commit suicide by their hands but no one was taking him up. "Riders! Rollers! Don't no one want no smoke! Scary ass niggas!"

Carey checked and berated the dorm full of killers but no one killed him. Instead they just simply ignored him like any one of the many flies flying around the dorm. Most eventually retreated to their cells to escape him. He roamed the cell house for hours until it was time to lock down for the night.

"You want smoke?" Carey dared his bunkmate when he entered the cell.

"Hell naw!" he said and raised his hands in surrender. He was one of the few civilians in the dorm and had enough smoke for a lifetime.

"See these bitches scared of me," Carey nodded and stretched out on his bunk. It would be his home until the next van took the condemned convicts to prison.

"Naw, actually," the kid began, then paused.

"Actually what?" Carey demanded and stood for conflict.

"Someone with some pull told them to stand down," he explained. Whoever it was had enough pull to pump the brakes on both gangs at the same time. "Word is, you bet not get a pimple in dis bih!"

"Hmp," he huffed and wondered. He racked his brain to figure out who he knew with that kind of pull. It was more than pull, it took a mighty yank to spare his life. Only one person came to mind and his head shook from side to side. "My damn daddy."

"Shit, see if he can keep these niggas off my ass too!" the killer pleaded. He may have been a killer and all but even killers get tired of getting their ass kicked. The gangs would keep kicking that ass until he joined one or the other.

"That nigga ain't do that shit to help me," Carey chuckled dryly. "Nah, that nigga wanna see me do all this time."

"Damn! That's fucked up," his celly moaned and shook his head along with him. A week later they were shipped off to serve their time.

THE COURT DATES kept coming but no one was going to jail for this next one. This was the civil suite Marquita filed against the booster and his Key man insurance policy. Jim Hartwell had argued that he had significant investment in the kid. What he couldn't explain was the wagers he made that West View would win the state championship.

"Taking your 'investment' into consideration..." the lady judge began. She made air quotes with her fingers to show what she thought of his argument.

"Uh-oh," Jim's attorney sighed since he didn't like the look or sound of that. He liked the case even less since even he thought it was slightly slimy to insure the kid since he was from the ghetto.

"And, you listed the relationship as nephew," the judge continued and turned to Marquita next to her lawyer at the next table.

"Looks like your mom is going to kick some butt," Carey told their son Mark from the galley. He softly bounced his knee to rock the newborn.

"Is Jim Hartwell your brother ma'am?" the judge asked even though Stevie Wonder would be able to see they weren't related.

"Ion know him!" she said and rolled her neck for effect. Mainly because she liked the way it affected her man. Carey loved her ghetto talk even though she rarely used it any more. Usually when he was digging her out real good. That ghetto talk always made him dig deeper.

"I didn't think so. That's why I'm awarding you three million dollars from the policy. As well as the home he gifted you for your son," the judge said and banged her gavel. That meant she said what she said so she stood.

"We won!" Marquita cheered and cheesed when she rushed back to her family. She retrieved her baby from her baby daddy and nuzzled his cheek. "We won baby! Your big brother is still taking care of his mama."

"We're not done winning!" Carey said and called for the judge before she got away. "Excuse me, your honor!"

"Yes?" the woman wondered since he was with the winning party.

"Can I get you to marry us before you leave?" he asked to

Marquita's surprise. She was so elated to be asked she never gave much thought to an actual wedding. It was enough just to look at the fancy ring he gave her.

"I would be honored!" the woman cheered and waved them over. The bailiff and stenographer would serve as witnesses for the last second nuptials. A few minutes later the judge used the powers vested in her to pronounce them man and wife. "You may now kiss the bride!"

"Told you, you would get your happily ever after," Carey reminded and kissed his bride.

"You did," she sighed in between kisses. This was the end of their story and her happily ever after.

The End

EPILOGUE

"C-note in this bitch! One of y'all niggas get up!" C-note barked when barged into the prison barber shop. To his surprise his dad's protective custody had followed him down the road. Everyone one of the convicts who rode with him had been flipped one way or another in the week they had been there.

One had become a Rider, two others had joined the Rollers. Both of the white men who rode with them were now white women. Walking around like Bruce Jenner in dresses and fake boobs. Meanwhile, no one dared to even look his way. That's why when he received a slip to visit the barber shop he barged in like a bear.

"I got you player," a barber said and pulled the sheet from his half finished client.

"Man!" the man pouted as he sat down and waited to get the other half of his head cut. The banal barbershop talk resumed once Carey was seated. They talked about the usual subjects of pussy, drugs, money and murder. Subjects Carey knew all about.

"Shit, I prolly fucked more hoes than all y'all broke ass niggas put together!" he laughed. He always enjoyed talking down on people but it was even sweeter since they couldn't do anything about it. "Y'all niggas ain't never had no white girl head! Y'all niggas ain't no killers! I been knocking niggas off..."

Carey lost his train of thought and nearly choked on his next words when a familiar face walked into the barbershop. His presence was larger than life and pushed the rest of the men right out of the room. Carey tried to get up himself but the barber's strong arms easily held him in place.

"Un-uh, finish your story," the man said as he took a seat right in front of him.

"I, I, I mean," Carey stammered. Big Marquis looked so much like his son there was no question of who he was. What he didn't know was why he was here. "You know my dad said no one can touch me!"

"Nah, I spared you lil nigga," Marquis corrected and pulled a phone from his pocket. He placed his video call and leaned back. "Finish your story..."

"Hello?" Marquita asked and scrunched her face up when she saw her baby daddy on the phone. They didn't have a baby anymore so she wondered why he was calling. She cast a glance out at her husband flipping steaks on the grill.

"Yeah, this nigga was just telling us about how he killed our kid," he explained. Marquita knew who he was and what was about to happen. She nodded her head and leaned in to watch.

Marquis gave the nod and the barber produced a straight razor. He started from one ear and pulled it around his neck to the other ear. Carey looked shocked but nothing happened for a few full seconds. The thin line suddenly opened up and blood gushed from the now gaping wound.

Carey made a gruesome blood curdling sound as blood spewed down his shirt. Marquita didn't blink as she watched him struggle for life while the barber held him in place. The light in his eyes flickered before it went dark. His head dropped to his chest as his soul gurgled out from the wound.

Marquis flipped the phone to see Marquita's face. She wore a pleasant smile and nodded. He nodded back and disconnected the call.

"Are you ok?" Carey senior asked when he found Marquita staring off into space.

"Huh? Oh, yeah. I am now," she cheered and kissed his lips to prove it. Now she really could have her happily ever after....

STAY TUNED for To Love and Die in Atlanta, vol 3

IN THE MEANTIME, check out Bad Cop...

BAD COP

By

Sa'id Salaam

I hate funerals. Any funeral but especially cop funerals, they are the worse. A bunch of phony mother fuckers rejoicing that it was you instead of them laying in that box. Then, what's up with the kilts and bag pipes? Like all cops are Irish or some shit. Then your so-called brothers all misty eyed even though racism is alive and kicking in the force. Department preacher singing your praises no matter if you were straight as an arrow or crooked as a fish hook. Most of these guys and gals need to be in jail themselves. That vice detective in the front row got the biggest child porn collection in the Tristate area. The lady cop next to him sell more pussy than the law allows. The so-called drug taskforce got more dope in the street than the cartel but, who am I to talk huh? Just look at the position I got myself into. Laid out with my academy picture beside a closed casket. You know it's ugly when they have to close the lid on you.

Yeah, I hate funerals, especially cop funerals, especially when it's mine.

CHAPTER 1

I came along way from a happy, chubby girl growing up in a big house on Long Island to a dead cop in Atlanta. Most New Yorkers move south to slow down, prosper and live. Not me, nope. I came down here, got in a whole bunch of trouble and got my ass killed. It's a long story so let's start from the beginning.

"HOW'S MY BABY!" Officer Rohan Robinson sang as he came out of the bedroom dressed in his uniform. His east Indian heritage gave his skin a nice golden tone while his hair was almost straight. His dark skin wife Michelle knew the combination would make some pretty children but more importantly have good hair.

She envisioned a bunch of handsome, curly-headed boys, but all she got was one daughter. A pretty, little girl who would never need a perm but still, boys are not the same as girls. She came from a household of five boys and her being the lone girl. She saw how different her parents treated her from them. She went from wanting to be a boy to wanting nothing but boys.

"Hey baby I..." Michelle began but Rohan wasn't talking to her and scooped up their daughter Megan instead.

"Hey daddy!" the little girl squealed in delight as he blew raspberries on her chubby cheeks. The happy child had skin tone exactly like her dads and big, black, bouncy curls for hair. Being an only child, spoiled by her father made her a fat but happy child. Michelle wore a jealous scowl at playing second fiddle but quickly erased it when Rohan turned her way.

"And my darling wife?" he greeted extending his arm so she could join the group hug.

They had just quietly made love before he showered and dressed for his night shift. Their theme song 'just in case I don't make it home tonight' would play in the background to ensure their child didn't hear the moans and groans of her pursuit of another child. He could get some more when he got home since their daughter would be off to school.

"Last but not least," she quipped as she joined the embrace. Megan reached to squeeze her neck as well. The gifted 7-year-old was smart enough to notice the temperature change whenever her father left. What she couldn't add, subtract or multiply but saw her mother was jealousy over her. She was too young to understand what it was but sure felt it.

"You know I love my ladies don't you?" he asked needlessly. He proved his love and devotion to his family on a regular basis.

He secured them a big house out on Long Island that seemed to be a million miles away from the south Bronx projects they came from. Two brand new cars in the driveway and closets full of clothes. Rohan made it his mission in life to protect and serve but that started at home with his family first. Being overextended forced him to work several double shifts each week.

"Yes!" they sang in chorus and squeezed him again. He closed his eyes and basked in the love before heading out into the dangerous streets of Harlem.

"Love you guys. See you in the morning." he proclaimed and gave each a parting kiss. Michelle blushed knowing just how he would see her when he got in. Both smiled and waved as he exited the house and entered his car. They kept smiling and waving until he was out of sight.

"Wanna watch a movie with me?" Megan turned and asked hopefully before the temperature dropped.

"Nah," Michelle said turning up the corner of her lip. It really wasn't the child's fault that she reminded her of the stuck up pretty girls who taunted her about dark skin and course hair. It definitely wasn't her fault that she gave birth to her and not the brood of sons she longed for. She just couldn't seem to get pregnant again even though they had sex daily.

Mother and daughter went their separate ways to do their separate thing. For the girl that meant the daunting task of trying to figure out which toys to play with. She had Barbie this and Barbie that, not to mention every video game system available in those days. The smarts child's number one past time was the encyclopedia set. Just something else for her ratchet mother to talk about.

Michelle went and got on the phone with her friend Reese back in the Bronx. The two had grown up together in the same projects. They smoked the same weed, wore the same clothes and slept with the same dudes. Michelle happen to catch Rohan's eye in a club and the rest was history. She would have slept with him that first night but he had school the next day. He was so busy they didn't get a chance to hang out for a couple of weeks. Once the nerd from Queens got a taste of a hoe from the Bronx he was hooked. He proposed weeks later.

Reese was still doing the same thing resulting in four baby daddies and a case of genital warts. They didn't get to hang out much but spoke almost daily. Michelle loved to brag about her husband, house, car and life. Reese always congratulated her but secretly despised her.

"So, Rohan just upgraded my truck. You know you need an SUV out here in the suburbs. You're so lucky to still be in the projects. Bus stop right out in front and you can always catch a gypsy cab." Michelle bragged and dissed at the same time. Two fucked up people can never really be friends but they can relate.

"Mmhm," Reese hummed since she was holding in smoke from the blunt she was smoking. She laced it with powdered cocaine to make the high, higher and last longer. Some call it a 'Woolie' or 'dirty' but it should be called 'Strike one' on the way to striking out. Most crack heads start off light like this. Then, get a stripe and graduate to the pipe, aka strike three.

"So what you been up to girl?" she asked knowing there wasn't shit to be up to in the projects. Old folks still lived there because it was all they could afford. They just waited on their reservation to the upper room. The young ones with vision escaped and never came back. The others sold drugs and made babies, also waiting to die.

"Just chilling. My baby daddies coming through with that check so I been straight. Hitting the club err night," she relayed between tokes.

Michelle could hear her smoking and wished she could get a pull. Just one long toke, and a line. Just one long, thick line of coke. Oh and a big swig from a 40 like back in the days. She twisted her lips ruefully, knowing that wasn't going to happen. Not with a cop for a husband. Not just a cop but one of Manhattan's best narcotic cops.

Meanwhile Megan read two books at the same time. One was for school and the other just because she loved to read. Books were like an all-expense paid vacation to wherever. She'd already visited 15 countries on 3 different continents. Her actions and adventures were nothing compared to what her father had going on.

CHAPTER 2

"Sup 'potna. You love that monkey suit I see!" Rohan's much younger partner Jackson greeted as he entered the locker room. The light skin pretty boy dressed like the rapper/rock star he envisioned himself as.

"My daughter loves my uniform," he replied as he began to change out of it. It was partially true since Megan did love to see her hero in uniform, but he loved wearing it just as much. He was proud to be a New York city police officer. Even after his promotion to detective and plain clothes he still wore his blues every chance he got.

"I need to swing through and see my kid," he said like he only had one. He made almost as many babies as he did arrest but only counted the one by his main chick. A hot-blooded Puerto Rican with a hot head and even hotter vagina. Their tumultuous relationship revolved around fighting, fucking and shopping.

"Yeah," Rohan grunted and bit his tongue. He couldn't imagine not seeing his beautiful daughter every day. That's why he worked so hard to make sure he came home every night. Just another example of how incompatible he and Jackson were.

'Jax' was a cowboy. A rooting, tooting, two gun shooting cowboy. They were in the middle of a big undercover operation that would get them both either promoted or dead. A win/win since either way he wouldn't have to work with the man anymore. He may have not seen the man take money but it was obvious. Unfortunately, it was the rule and not the exception. Why should the dope boys have all the fun with all the money, cars and women?

"So, Snake wants to meet us at Back Shots!" Jax cheered rubbing his hands together like dinner was served. It was a high-end strip club known for having the baddest bad girls in the city.

"Why not City Island? Lobster and crabs?" Rohan wanted to know. He was a married man and hated being around a bunch of women. Especially some of the baddest bad girls in the city completely naked. He could see himself speeding home in the morning to rush inside of his wife for relief. Michelle would of course complain about him smelling like baby oil with glitter on his face.

"Or...Back Shot, big titties and fat asses. Blow jobs and shit. Bet Michelle gives you killer blow jobs!" he cheered.

"Jax you obviously can't see it, but there's a line, and you crossed it." Rohan calmly explained. He knew his partner well enough to know most of his words came straight out his mouth without ever passing through his brain. A normal person's brain will filter inappropriate shit and allow a person to keep it to themselves.

"My bad! I know you married guys are sensitive. Tender dicks, nothing wrong with that." he offered. It was probably as close as he could get to an actual apology so Rohan let it be.

"No problem. You ready?" he asked after transforming into his street clothes and persona. His Indian looks got him called 'Tonto' as a child coming up. It was the wrong kind of Indian but he embraced it. He looked every bit the part in a tailored suite and chunky platinum jewelry.

Jax on the other hand lived the part 24/7. He didn't have to change clothes because he dressed like a dope boy every day. Complete with an easy hundred grand worth of jewels dripping from his neck, ears, fingers and wrist. He pushed a spanking new STS Caddie but had a Porsche parked at his Brooklyn condo.

"Gotta take a quick shit," he said holding up a finger. He did that quite often making his partner assume he had a digestive problem. He had a problem alright but it wasn't IBS.

Rohan rushed into a stall and shimmied out of his skinny pants and silk drawers. He sat his bare ass cheeks down on the toilet and dug into his pocket. His pretty smile spread on his handsome face when he saw the glistening cocaine in a hundred-dollar bill. That smile turned into a grimace as he took a heaping scoop up each nostril.

"Argh! This shit is the shit!" he congratulated. He knew he came up on some fish scale when they busted a dealer in Washington Heights. The coke was so pretty he grabbed a few handfuls to keep for himself. That and twenty grand from the pile of money.

"Straight now?" Rohan asked when he returned. He noticed an extra ping and zip in the man but knew a good shit can do that.

"Super straight!" he shot back, super high. He followed his partner out of the precinct into the parking lot. A press of a key fob made a Lexus beep in response. "Piece of shit they got us riding in."

"The Lexus?" Rohan shot back in shock. He knew full well it started at ninety grand because Michelle just tried to talk him into buying one. Jax was right because she did have some killer head, she threw in that morning to help her campaign. In the end, she had to settle on a new truck but that was close to sixty.

"Jap crap! You gotta drive the new Porsche!" he shot back and climbed behind the wheel.

"Still, be easy," he recommended since he drove like a bat out of hell. The last thing they needed was to get pulled over by other cops, which could blow their cover.

"I got this," he assured him as he eased out of the parking lot. As soon as he hit the street he mashed the gas and drove like a bat out of hell out to the Bronx...

Made in the USA
Columbia, SC
23 August 2022